# VENUS RISING

## DATE DUE

| | |
|---|---|
| | |
| | |
| | |
| | |
| | |
| | |
| | |
| | |
| | |
| | |
| | |
| | |
| | |
| | |
| | |
| | |

PRINTED IN U.S.A.

D1056228

# VENUS RISING

Pamela Hill

**CHIVERS**
**THORNDIKE**

This Large Print edition is published by BBC Audiobooks Ltd, Bath, England and by Thorndike Press®, Waterville, Maine, USA.

Published in 2004 in the U.K. by arrangement with United Writers Publications Ltd.

Published in 2004 in the U.S. by arrangement with United Writers Publications Ltd.

U.K. Hardcover   ISBN 0–7540–6965–6  (Chivers Large Print)
U.K. Softcover   ISBN 0–7540–6966–4  (Camden Large Print)
U.S. Softcover   ISBN 0–7862–6617–1  (Nightingale)

The text of this Large Print edition is unabridged.
Other aspects of the book may vary from the original edition.

Set in 16 pt. New Times Roman.

Printed in Great Britain on acid-free paper.

**British Library Cataloguing in Publication Data available**

**Library of Congress Control Number: 2004103819**

For V.J.F.

# Part One

# CHAPTER ONE

The ungodly old squire of Leys, Sir Eldred Seaborne, who it had always been assumed would come to a worse end than dying in bed, was doing so at last of a second apoplexy, his port-wine countenance propped up by pillows. Beside the bed, by contrast, his lawyer, scribbling down the terms of the belated Will, was lean and blanched as a stick of celery left out of the daylight on purpose. He had been called to Leys hurriedly from London, and hoped his client would not expire before signing as it would lead to immense complications with all and sundry.

It had several times been suggested to Sir Eldred that he make a Will, but he had driven off the persons concerned with language seldom encountered now in polite circles in the present genteel century. His age was seventy-two, and, with one thing and another, it was a wonder he had reached it. He had first seen the light in the year of George III's coronation.

In plain fact it had entertained the squire to keep everyone waiting as long as possible about his intentions. One reason was that, like many, he could not bring himself to believe that he would ever die. The second was that his wife, who never now came downstairs—it

3

was some years now since he had set eyes on her—had borne him no heirs. This was her fault. His own bastard progeny adequately staffed Leys House itself, the stables, and the farms. The town, up the hill after a flat mile, had proved less amenable, as the sour-faced townsfolk, changed hardly at all in outlook since Cromwell's day, kept a firm eye on their wives, daughters, maidservants, and the stranger within their gates.

In other words, the only legitimate relative left was Sir Eldred's great-nephew Gareth, who was the kind of feller that shot his foxes. He had been sent to Cambridge, then announced that he wanted to become a damned poet. To discourage this, he'd been packed off to keep the books for the factor on Sir Eldred's Irish estates, like many bestowed by the Wisest Fool in Christendom to any settler prepared to take on a patch of bog somewhere in the middle of that unchancy island. Sir Eldred had never been there, though he relied partly on the rents sent by successive, and unpopular, factors.

The occupation hadn't done young Gareth any good; for one thing he had had the impudence to dismiss the current factor, saying the man was lining his pockets at the expense of the tenantry, whose roofs nevertheless continued to leak. Shortly thereafter, Gareth had married, without any by-your-leave, a young bride whose father

4

edited some damned radical newspaper in the tradition of Jonathan Swift. Unless the O'Tooles had been kings of Ireland once like all the rest, young Stella—that was the filly's name—had no ancestry anyone had ever heard of. So far, to make it worse, the couple, though married now three years, had no children. Gareth probably couldn't manage it. He had been a gangling sort of a boy who wrote his damned poetry instead of taking a look at the local girls here at Leys; he probably hadn't a notion how to get on with the business as it should be done. That the line of the celebrated Sir Posthumus Seaborne, whose father had been killed in the Royalist wars and his mother manhandled by Cromwellian soldiery, causing her to die in premature childbirth, should end after only two centuries was lamentable. Sir Posthumus had grown up understandably small, but tough, and at the age of eleven, when the King came home, had knocked out two of Old Noll's teeth with a well-aimed brick as the latter's corpse, dug up after a year, had hung festering on the public gallows. Young Posthumus' feat had endeared the boy so greatly to Charles II that that monarch ensured repayment of his late father's Royalist fines not once, but multiplied by four. Given the fact that most Puritan inhabitants of Leys had hung on to their ill-gotten gains in this way and prospered, the end result was a rich squire and a rich town council, disliking each other's ways heartily. This view still pertained, especially as Sir Posthumus' son and successor, who had been Sir Eldred's great-grandfather, had had the foresight to advise Sir Robert Walpole on no account to invest in the South Sea Bubble. His reward had been prodigious, and its effects lasting.

In plain words, there was plenty of money, even after Sir Eldred's own unedifying career. The title and lands were of course entailed, but the money wasn't. It was his to do with as he liked, and he still wasn't entirely sure what he did like. Mrs Stevens, the housekeeper, who had obliged in various ways including the bearing to himself of the eventual second footman, ought perhaps to have a little something. As for his wife, through whose considerable dowry Sir Eldred had roystered in various ways best not specified, he supposed she ought to have a jointure, otherwise it would look odd. None of the bastards need receive more than their accustomed wages, as otherwise everything would be used up.

No, it had best be Gareth, provided he fathered an heir. Better still, make it a male heir within five years of the marriage. That would keep both of them at it. Sir Eldred enunciated a term which caused the lawyer's paper-thin eyelids to lower themselves in professionally concealed distaste. These days, manners and conversation were no longer so coarse as formerly. He raised his head and regarded the dying squire through spectacles which enhanced his thin, prudently investigative nose.

'Assuming that there is no male heir, Sir Eldred, where is the money to go at the end of the stipulated period?'

Stipulated be damned. It was the kind of word these fellers enjoyed using. A sly grin intervened for moments between Sir Eldred and the already poised grim reaper. The townsfolk were subservient, as was proper, and would ring the passing-bell at his death and turn out in ostentatious mourning. Let them have what was left, by then, of the money. A condition must be that they erect a statue of himself, life-sized, in the market square round which, by a statute which had never been repealed, harlots were whipped half naked three times in public at the cart's tail. Sir Eldred had watched it happen once, with some diversion as the girl in question had, in the first place, been led from the straight and narrow by himself.

He contrived to sign the Will, wheezed twice, then died. The passing-bell shortly tolled its deep note, the metal itself having been forged in the reign of Henry VII and for some reason, not melted down between then and now. Informed of events in time for the funeral, the new squire, and his golden-haired wife, crossed the water and came home.

# CHAPTER TWO

The new squire was twenty-six. He was tall rather than short, and slim rather than sturdy. He had a pleasant open face, grey eyes, hair the colour of cinnamon, fine hands, fair skin, and an expression rather too grave for his age. As he had told his future father-in-law the editor when he asked for Stella's hand, he was not a romantic. Poets on the whole were unfaithful to their wives, and he himself would love none but Stella and if he might not marry her, would marry nobody.

'That would be a pity,' had said Brian O'Toole, and had given his permission with some relief. Although he had spared no expense in having Stella brought up as a fine lady, she was unlikely to become one unless in the event of some eccentric lord with liberal ideas walking into his newspaper office. This was exactly what had happened, as young Gareth Seaborne, unlike most, was concerned with the fate of the tenants on his great-uncle's Irish estates, till now administered by the customary crooked factor dear to absentee landlords. Tuberculosis, starvation, leaking roofs and a diet of potatoes were the tenants' lot, and the rents which found their way across to Sir Eldred in England were devoid of stated repairs which had never been carried out, while the difference stayed in the factor's pocket.

Gareth had seen fit to sack the factor and undertake the task himself, to the evident wrath of his great-uncle, who told him to stop poking his gormless nose into what didn't yet concern him. However the old reprobate admitted that he was receiving more money than hitherto, whether or not the wretched peasants knew any benefit. It was to discuss ideas he entertained for their better fate that Gareth had ventured to call in person at the office of the *Laracor Tribune,* and outside encountered the bluest pair of eyes he had ever seen, falling in love instantly. Miss Stella, her maid and her little dog had happened to come downstairs for their walk just as he arrived, a state of affairs which influenced all their futures.

Now, he was driving with golden-haired Stella—her colouring had no doubt come from some viking ancestor who, most respectably, had long ago opened up a market in Dublin while his peers were still raping and raiding— towards the newly fronted manor of Leys after the old squire's pompous funeral. Of necessity, they were both dressed in black, but black only made Stella look more beautiful than ever, setting off her rose-petal complexion and the piled bright hair, seen below a velvet mourning-hat with the abandonment of a heron's feather pinned on to tug in the wind.

She had sat in the carriage while what remained of Sir Eldred was bestowed in the ugly modern Perpendicular Gothic vault built halfway up the hill; women didn't attend such ceremonies. Gareth had of course gone in, and had reflected during proceedings on how he hadn't really wanted to move to Leys as its squire at all, but Stella had thought of it as an exciting adventure. 'Dublin's dull,' she had said. 'It's all very well for you, my darling, but you're hardly ever in town, out with the tenants half your life as you are. I want to see more of you.' She added that she had heard Leys House and the gardens were very fine, and much better for the health than town. That last point had decided him; the Dublin house was damp, and perhaps at Leys they could produce the required child. He could always cross from Pembroke to keep an eye now and again, and Daniel O'Toole, Stella's uncle, lived now in the dismissed factor's house on Raheere estate. Dan was a liberal like his brother, and believed in the rights of the poor.

Certainly the manor here, built at first from stones rifled from the old abbey at the Dissolution, and altered since, reared gleaming in the summer sunlight as they bowled along the flat last mile between the house and town. In front, ready with a reception and speeches, waited a darkly forbidding cloud of town councillors, headed by the high sheriff, a man disliked by many but feared by all. The civic rules left on the statute book gave him unlimited powers, as geography, in the form of marsh and forest, had isolated Leys from the rest of England, and her townspeople were still brought up almost in terms of the long-dead Commonwealth. The sheriff was a tall solidly built man whose thick powerful thighs, not to mention his voracious testicles, were concealed by the sad-hued robes of his office, bright colours still being suspect as frivolous in the town of Leys. It wouldn't have been proper for civil dignitaries to wear anything at all light, or encouraging to levity. That the sheriff was known to have a sedulous history of seduction of helpless young females remained unmentioned. The correction-house was up the hill.

\*     \*     \*

'They look a glum lot, I must say; perhaps it's the occasion,' said Stella. Gareth turned his head to look at her again, to the slight danger of the horses.

'They always look like that,' he said absently. A clanging and clashing had begun, as had always by tradition happened at the squire's arrivals and departures from Leys. It consisted of cooking-pots banged on ploughshares, and trumpets blown with more

11

enthusiasm than talent. The whole thing had been a tradition since the Restoration, when Sir Posthumus had at last come home.

'What a noise,' said Stella, remembering it earlier at the funeral. 'Were they so very fond of your great-uncle?' She had never set eyes on the old squire, and rather wished she had. He would have been more entertaining than this assembly of pompous black-clad crows. She caught the high sheriff's eye, and found it full of unbridled lust. He didn't look like a person one wanted to know.

'They disapproved of him profoundly, but there was nothing they could do about it. He was by far too rich, and could checkmate them by bribes.'

'*We* won't be able to do that unless we have a son by the year after next. Let's spend the money in advance.'

'Don't laugh, darling, it's never allowed in the town. What a noise! I'm going to stop it in future. Let me help you down.'

A man in livery had come to take the horses away. Stella decided he looked like a rat. There was no need to be fanciful, however; it was simply after having seen that sheriff. She wouldn't like to be in his power. They advanced arm-in-arm, she and Gareth, to hear the speeches. These were long, dull and hypocritical, as might have been expected of men whose surnames had once been, in the high sheriff's case, Stern-in-the-vengeance-of-the-Lord's-wrath, now shortened understandably to keep up with the times. His other name was Hezekiah, and he preached extempore lay sermons on Sundays to which everyone must come whether they liked it or not. He might almost have been preaching one now. However his cold grey-green gaze, which had terrified many young women into subjection, rested without apology on the beguiling shape of Stella's breasts beneath her gown. One day, in some manner, he would get the new squire's lady beneath him, like the rest. She needn't set herself up.

\*       \*       \*

Gareth had stopped listening and was remembering Ireland. Before his marriage to the girl named after Swift's beloved, no doubt to express her father's ideals, he had had constructive notions of his own about founding a cottage industry at Raheere when he had the money. There were talents to be found among the thin-faced tenants, as he had noted during a chance encounter with a scrawny young girl seated by a smoky peat fire in her father's cottage, working, with a grimy length of thread once white, to produce a miracle.

It was going to be a piece of lace in rose-and-shamrock pattern, she told him, that the Carmelite nuns had taught her while she was with them as her mother had wanted, but she hadn't had the vocation and left after two years. If only there was more thread she could finish it. She hadn't thought of selling it, and Gareth, in his brief courtship of Stella before they married, promised the girl that if he bought her a new ball of linen thread, and she finished the lace as a collar, he would buy it and pay her, and would see that others bought more of her work. It was the first step of the enterprise; later, he'd persuaded a cobbler to come for a salary, to teach the men how to make boots and shoes out of calfskin and pigskin, so now they could afford to eat some of their own veal and pork. As for the women, they made lace once they knew how, or spun the wool that hadn't till then been allowed out of Ireland, as the English were jealous of their trade. Homespun cloaks, dyed in magical colours coaxed from bog-herbs and plants and bark, sold well in Dublin once the fashion started. Stella in person had helped to start it, and the sight of her walking down O'Connell Street in a cape of vegetable green, escorted by himself, had set the town talking and made it buy. By now, a shop had been rented two doors down from the *Tribune* office, calling itself Laracor Industries. Laracor had been the first clerical charge of Jonathan Swift, who despite his bitter resentment at having been banished long ago to Ireland, had done his best for the underprivileged there. Brian O'Toole had always been inspired by his

14

writings, and had named the *Tribune* in his honour. Laracor itself was a small place within riding distance of Dublin.

Gareth had been remembering all of that, and how he must soon make a return visit, hard as it was to leave Stella. However she would enjoy being the lady of the manor, with its new front in the classical mode, and its artificial lake with swans and waterfowl and a weeping willow, and the strutting peacocks, and the gardens laid out by a pupil of Capability Brown, and the field beyond. He himself was interested in agriculture and wanted to inspect the home farm tomorrow. If only the speeches could be done with! They wanted to refresh themselves and go in to dinner; it had been a long journey.

*     *     *

One other inmate had sat at the back of the carriage; Stella's maid Pilar, who was half Spanish. She was not notable in any other way, being small and sallow, with lank dark hair scooped up into a bun beneath her cap. She had small dark eyes which missed nothing and small unremarkable features, and was dutiful and clean. One cotton-gloved hand rested on Miss Stella's, that was my lady's, jewel-box, with which she had been entrusted and inside which, she knew, reposed the pearl necklace Sir Gareth had bought his wife lately, with

15

matching bracelets to adorn her white arms. Beyond was a space where the little dog, a white French poodle named Talley, should have sat, but he had been run over and killed by a drunken carriage-driver in Dublin last year, and Miss Stella had cried her heart out. It was her first sorrow, as she didn't remember her mother and had always been protected and made much of.

Pilar had not. However she could just remember her own mother, who had been brought home as his wife by a much older sergeant from the Peninsular campaign. They had spoken Castilian together and she still remembered a little. Then the *madre* had run off with somebody and Pilar's father said you could understand it, he was in bad health with his war wound and her mother had had to look after herself. He added that he was taking Pilar to the orphanage because he hadn't got long. 'They'll train you there for service,' he said. 'It's better than nothing, and if an employer knows he can trust you, you'll rise high.'

She had never forgotten that, because he died a few weeks after she had been admitted to a bleak place smelling of harsh soap, rags and sour poverty-stricken sweat. She was made, like the others, to earn her keep, scrub and clean and launder and iron and starch and mend. After three years of it she had a certificate to show she was indentured in the

Art, Trade and Mystery of a Servant, and was apprenticed to a worthy and eminent citizen of the town, who repeatedly raped her. After it happened the fourth time Pilar ventured to go and tell her mistress, a lady who sat comfortably upholstered in her drawing-room; and was told she was a liar and a bad girl, and must have been with men, and that if she spoke like that about Mr Greenbody again she should taste the birch, and would thereafter be returned to the orphanage with a bad character, so her next employment would not be as pleasant.

Rather than face what that meant, Pilar decided to run away. She had no money, as what she earned was returned to the orphanage until she had fully repaid her keep there. When she saw a hay-cart in the road she hid in it, with no idea where it might be going. She stayed in it three days and nights, not daring to get out when the driver stopped for something to eat; if you stole a loaf you could be sent to Australia. Pilar chewed on shreds of hay; after all, horses lived on it.

The cart stopped to unload at last, and Pilar wormed her way out without being seen, running off down filthy streets in whatever place they had come to. The gutters were full of garbage and stinking offal, and she knew how the Prodigal Son must have felt, but she hadn't any father to return to. Thin folk as hungry as herself stood about, ragged and begging; one very old woman played a harp with her withered fingers for farthings passers-by threw, catching them expertly and going on with her plucking of the strings. The sound followed Pilar as she went, no longer running now because with luck, she'd been lost by anyone who might be searching. It had begun to rain, and she wondered what happened to the old woman's tune if her harp-strings got soggy with the wet. She herself was soaked, her clothes and hair full of wisps of hay. She knew she looked like a beggar or a madwoman, and once when there was a passing cow, with servants bringing cans to fill with its warm fresh milk, she begged for a drink. 'Off with you,' they said, and one man kicked Pilar away, hurting her shin. It was growing dark, and in the end she collapsed and lay in the nearest doorway, hiding herself in its shadows, much afraid. If she didn't eat she would die, and it didn't much matter. Her shin still throbbed where the servant with the can had kicked her. It wasn't the worst thing that could happen, here in the street.

Luckily she was unmolested, and lay there till dawn and beyond. At least Mr and Mrs Greenbody didn't know where to find her and tell the orphanage. She didn't know where she was, or even that she was in Dublin.

After the light grew a tall man and a girl came to the entry and saw Pilar lying there. She hadn't the strength to move; she was stiff with lying out all night. The tall man had a kind face. 'Please, sir, do you need a servant?' she asked him, adding that she could iron and wash and mend so's you couldn't see the difference. 'I'd only want food,' she said, and fainted for the first and last time in her life.

Brian O'Toole carried her inside.

That was how she'd become Miss Stella's maid. Most people would not have taken her on trust without her certificate, but Mr O'Toole wasn't like most people. Later on, after she'd had hot soup and some bread, he heard her story and said he would pay off the orphanage to leave her in peace, and if she could iron his daughter's petticoats she would be doing everyone a good turn, as they had a great many frills.

Pilar, seeing Miss Stella for the first time through tears of relief, knew she would never again set eyes on anyone as beautiful. Miss Stella was like an angel in church from *madre's* day, except that she laughed a great deal and angels probably didn't. There was no doubt she was spoilt, but after Mrs Greenbody it didn't matter. Miss Stella had always been given everything she wanted, to make up for the fact that her mother was dead; pretty clothes, velvet for winter with matching bonnets and a sealskin muff; muslin or silk for summer, with straw hats trimmed with artificial flowers that might almost have been real, and her golden hair and lovely face

19

looking out from under. She had just left the fashionable seminary for young ladies to which she had been sent, with all the extras like dancing and painting in water-colours and playing the pianoforte, except that she wasn't very good at the last, not being musical. It was a pleasure to starch and iron her frilly petticoats and look after the dresses, and be talked to like a friend rather than a servant. Stella's father had taught her that everybody was the same, that there was no such thing as high rank unless you deserved it, and that the least important people had rights whatever anyone said. This had caused the parents of the other young ladies at the fashionable school to avoid Stella, except at fashionable assemblies where everyone mingled, once having bought a ticket. 'I don't miss them at all,' said Stella. 'They couldn't talk about anything much, except getting married. Papa writes articles in his paper about how the poor people make butter and bring on bacon, but have to sell it to England and live on potatoes themselves. Then when there's a potato famine, as happened not long ago, they starve and die.'

It seemed doubtful for some time whether or not Miss Stella would get married, because her father's views were not shared by the rich and righteous who might otherwise have provided a suitable husband for somebody as beautiful, brought up a fine lady. Miss Stella played all day with her little dog, or strummed inexpertly on the piano, or glued shells on a box, and once a morning and again in an evening, if it was fine, would go out with Pilar and Talley on his scarlet lead, wagging his tail, for a walk.

That was when they met the handsome young man, slim and fashionably dressed, who had been about to enter Mr O'Toole's office when they came downstairs, but noticed Miss Stella at once and she noticed him. It was like a spark struck between them, and after that the young man called almost every day.

Nobody had noticed Pilar, but she hadn't expected it. She held the little dog carefully, his white fluffy coat washed and brushed by herself, his red lead wound round her wrist, his small warm body close against her bodice. They went for the walk, and she kept Talley out of the dirt of the gutters. She loved him as much as Miss Stella did, and soon she loved Miss Stella's young man as well, but kept it to herself. He was so gentle and kind, although quite young; and of course very handsome, and in line for a title; that last didn't matter.

\*     \*     \*

Soon he and Miss Stella were married, and she made a beautiful bride. It made less difference in ways than it might have done, as Mr O'Toole wouldn't let Miss Stella go and live

where
Mr Gareth stayed in the factor's house at Raheere during the week; the land was boggy there and she might catch a fever, not to mention lice from the unfortunate tenants. Mr O'Toole's views were less practical than ideal, but there it was. So Mrs Stella, as she was now, stayed on at the Dublin house above the office, and Mr Gareth used to come and stay from Friday to Monday. During part of the time he and Mr O'Toole would discuss the growing prospect of Laracor Industries, and when they acquired the premises Pilar dusted and cleaned the shop and later, helped to dress the windows. The things in it were beautiful; more of the lace, like the collar Mrs Stella wore with her rose-coloured gown, and Pilar washed and ironed it carefully, and the rest of the trousseau as well. There was handwoven stuff and boots and shoes and even gloves, which had to be of calfskin as no lady would ever be seen wearing anything else. Pilar herself, being only a servant, wore cotton ones and knew she was lucky to have them.

Some of the Raheere tenants, Mr O'Toole admitted, were past saving and liked to distil their potatoes to make potheen and get drunk instead of eating, and mostly died young. However, after his brother, Mr Daniel, came to help with the business it got off to a fine start, and was beginning to pay for its rent when Mr Gareth's great-uncle, the one in

England with the title, died, and Mr Gareth became a Sir and Mrs Stella Lady Seaborne. That was mud in the eye for all the people who'd looked down their noses at her for being the daughter of a liberal editor.

Before then, Talley had been run over and killed.

*     *     *

Pilar knew it was her fault; she should have held on more tightly, but she'd been thinking about Sir Gareth and how he wouldn't like leaving Ireland and the new industry for long. Without warning Talley jumped from her arms and streaked, trailing his lead, across the road towards a lurcher bitch in heat and ready for anything. He never got there; on the way a passing carriage drove over him with a cracking sound, breaking his spine. He was dead by the time Pilar got there to pick him up. She held the limp mud-cluttered body against her, its head lolling; the carriage had driven on, a dog didn't matter. How was she to tell Miss Stella? She still thought of her as that. The tears were pouring down her own face, and she didn't cry as a rule. It must be her Irish side: the Spanish was hard as nails.

Luckily Sir Gareth had seen, and came to her. 'Don't trouble about it, Pilar,' he told her. 'I'll tell her a thief snatched him from your arms, and ran off and tripped in the road and

fell, and the dog escaped and was run over.'
Dreadful things happened to stolen pets, as
they both knew; a demand would be made for
money, and if it wasn't sent the dog's paws and
ears were sent back in a parcel. It was better
for Talley to be dead than that, and better for
Miss Stella if she heard it that way. As it was
she cried and cried, and Sir Gareth held her in
his arms, and said they'd go to England and
she would forget all about it soon in their new
life. They set off, and took Pilar with them,
and she was so grateful to Sir Gareth for
telling a slight lie on her behalf that she loved
him more than ever. She'd sat in the carriage
looking at the little peak in which his hair grew
at the back of his neck, and the fair flesh
beneath, like a little boy's. She was glad he and
Miss Stella were so happy together. The old
great-uncle had written a most unpleasant
letter at the time. Miss Stella said he'd made a
very odd Will since. Carrying the jewel-box
carefully, Pilar got out of the carriage after her
master and mistress. The gloomy delegation
had gone. The groom, if that was what he was,
who waited to take the carriage to the stables
didn't have a pleasant face; he looked like a
rat. There were a great many things no servant
must ever mention.

She found herself thinking, for no reason, of
what Dan O'Toole had told her about Stella's
mother.

He maybe shouldn't have done it: but he

hadn't many to confide in, being an old bachelor set in his ways. It hadn't been the whiskey with him, not that time. He was lonely, and fond of his brother, having regretted the marriage at the time.

'He was besotted by her. It suited him that she wasn't a lady. He has this notion fixed in his head that there should be no such thing as class.'

If he hadn't had the notion, he'd have left me in the doorway, Pilar thought. She saw Dan stare down at his glass and say 'After she ran off—'

'She ran off? Stella's mother?'

She shouldn't have spoken aloud, being a servant. However he went on, twisting the glass in his fingers. He had big square hands, a practical man's. He was a help with the printing.

'Stella was a baby, just able to crawl. She may just remember her mother: children remember more than you'd think. Maeve, that was her name, ran off with a scoundrel named O'Halloran. He'd been paying attention to her while my brother paid more to the paper. This O'Halloran'—Dan's voice roughened—'was in service with Lord Castlereagh, and that says enough in Ireland. They both came to a bad end, Maeve and her lover, and it was a judgment on her for leaving her child.'

'What happened?' asked Pilar, forgetting herself again and remembering *madre*.

Perhaps there had been a judgment on her as well: one didn't know. It made a link with Miss Stella, both of them losing their mother in the same way. Old Dan was still talking.

'My brother never got over it, or the death,' continued Dan. 'Their carriage overturned on the bad roads, lurching at speed with a drunk driver. Maeve broke her neck. O'Halloran saved his.'

He scowled. 'Brian was well rid of her,' he said. 'An adulteress, a coarse woman: he'd tried to be loyal. That's why he has been so particular to rear Stella as a fine lady, and we can only hope that her mother's blood won't out.'

'She is happy in her marriage,' said Pilar helpfully.

'Ah, you're a good girl, Pilar. You're intelligent, can put two and two together. You're no fool. Thankful my brother is at the marriage, and young Gareth like the son he never had.' The grey eyes brooded beneath the untidy whitening hair, and Dan O'Toole fell silent. His brother's wife had perhaps been the reason why he had remained a bachelor.

Pilar moved about, tidying the room. She was still thinking of her own father. He'd been generous when the *madre* ran off, saying she had to look after herself when she had the chance, knowing he was ill and wouldn't get better.

In the end, everyone had to look after

themselves. She'd had to: and must remember her own good fortune in being taken in here at all.

## CHAPTER THREE

'I did not think,' had said Brian O'Toole shortly after the marriage, seated in the Dublin house one evening twirling his own customary glass of whiskey, 'that I would have given my daughter to an Englishman, because the English should never have come to Ireland.'

It was a frequent statement of his when mildly under the influence, and Gareth, gazing at Stella who was seated smiling, in a blue dress, on the other side of the blazing hearth, smiled in return and said nothing. She made, he was thinking, a perfect picture with her white fingers round her little glass of ratafia, and her little white dog, a poodle, at her feet. He could not now imagine life without her, and scarcely listened to what the old gentleman was saying; they had both in any case heard it before.

'Take the cranes, now. They are beautiful creatures with long necks, and in the old days they were tame all over Ireland, for no one harmed them. Then the English king Henry II came over here to hide after the murder of

27

Becket, and lived in a wattle hut he'd built himself. He asked the Irish why they didn't roast and eat the cranes, and taught them that as well as other matters that did them no good. By the end of it there were too many greedy noblemen sent across, and no cranes left. If that was all he'd done, there would be less harm in it; but the pope, who had no business to do any such thing, granted him Ireland as a papal see. They had contrived well enough here since the coming of Christianity, which they brought with them after the Saxons, that is yourself, came to Britain, and drove the old races out in the end, to Ireland and Strathclyde and Wales and Brittany, and to this day the tongues can understand each other. A drop more, son-in-law?'

Gareth declined. He was temperate in all ways, and seldom drank spirits; the smoky Irish flavour did not displease him, however. 'Had you not given me your daughter, sir, I'd have carried her off,' he said, raising his glass to Stella. O'Toole scarcely heard him, so far away was he in ancient thought.

'There was no need for bishops at all; their abbots were enough, and the bishops were only made in order to cross the water and gain importance politically. We had our saints and our missionaries, as far as Germany, and one of them in the eighth century said the world was round, long before Columbus, but nobody remembers now.'

'A forebear of Stella's found America long before Columbus as well,' said Gareth, looking at her golden hair; it certainly showed viking ancestry, he had decided, and the vikings had settled in Dublin long ago and made it a port earlier than any. Her lashes and brows were not light, he was thinking, like many fair women's, but tipped naturally with a darker colour, seen against her cheeks as she slept. His love for her transformed him. It was because of Laracor Industries that Brian O'Toole had considered him as a son-in-law, and had talked early of his own idol Swift and how the dean had disliked Ireland thoroughly, but had done his best for the poor there.

'As few have since,' the old editor finished, setting down his glass with a thump. 'You and I do what we can. If everybody did what they could, and every man had a right to live on what he raises on his land, there would be no poverty. It's the injustice of the thing that makes my blood boil, and yours.' He could have gone on and on, and in the end, as always, everybody went to bed, and Stella let down her long golden hair for Gareth to brush, then bury his face in it before she plaited and tied it with white wool to keep it from tangling overnight. That way she looked like a schoolgirl, or else the prim Nordic maiden who had refused to give herself to a certain young man for nine nights. The latter had then described how if she would not agree to it, she

29

would be ravished at the gates of icy Hel by the lascivious god of frost and ice. In the end, for preference she had given herself to the young man for the nine nights he demanded.

'And what happened next?' asked Stella, plaiting her hair.

'According to the story, he then went away, and that was the end.'

'What an ungrateful young man. Do not you ever go away.'

'Never, never. Now I have you, I will stay much longer than nine nights.'

'Much, much longer. Oh, love me, love me, love me, love me.'

During the night he had a dream about tame Irish cranes. It seemed a pity they had killed them all. Gareth himself was fond of animals. The little white dog, Talley, still alive then, slept at the end of their bed, his small form curled up like that of a hedgehog. He followed Stella everywhere.

They had been happy again once he had comforted her for the dog's loss. He hoped they would be as happy at Leys. It was an entirely new way of life, and drove them somewhat in on themselves. He didn't much take to the townspeople or the hunting county, remembering both too well from a boy. He had nothing in common with them.

# CHAPTER FOUR

The long-established custom had taken place for the last time after the one when Sir Eldred's coffin was borne out of Leys House and up the hill to the mausoleum; the deafening sound of blown trumpets, cooking-pots beaten on ploughshares, and all other possible cacophony which had always happened when a squire of Leys travelled anywhere in his coach. Gareth, who intended buying an elegant cabriolet to drive himself and Stella into town with as little fuss as possible, ordained as promised that the noise should stop. He also had the late Sir Eldred's antique vehicle moved to the back of the stables, there to remain, and transferred the duties of the second footman to the care of the new carriage. The first footman had already asked permission to retire owing to varicose veins, a hazard due to standing all day.

'We don't need a footman,' Gareth told Stella. However, between that and the stopping of the trumpet-blasts and ploughshare-bangings, ill-feeling arose: Leys was being made to lose its face before the world. Mrs Stevens the housekeeper likewise asked permission to retire, as with the late squire's legacy she would manage to take a small house in town. In fact she was huffed because her son had not been promoted to first footman when the old one left. No doubt times were changing.

'I'm glad she's going,' said Stella. 'I didn't like her much, and I would sooner the son wasn't about the house. The coach-quarters are comfortable.' That was the young man with the face like a rat; no doubt he couldn't help it. She added that Pilar was more than capable of looking after the house. It would make everything much simpler to manage. She hadn't yet visited Sir Eldred's widow, and must do so soon; the old lady seldom received company, and had her own woman servant to look after her.

'Do exactly as you choose,' said Sir Gareth, gazing afresh on his wife's fair beauty; he could still never believe his luck in having obtained her. Shortly they went for their by now accustomed walk to feed the waterfowl, watch the brilliant peacocks, and admire the proudly gliding swans. A swan was such a clumsy sight when it waddled on land, yet superb above all others in the water. People were the same; they had their good side and their bad, he thought, all except Stella who was perfect. 'Tomorrow I must go round the farms,' he said; he hadn't been yet, and looked forward to it.

Stella wasn't interested in husbandry of that variety. 'You go there, and I'll visit the dowager,' she suggested. 'She must be ill; she didn't come down to greet us on our arrival.'

'She's never well; she is blind, and very old. It would be good of you, my darling. I only wish she could see you for herself.' Stella was wearing, today, a blue dress; it matched the colour of her eyes. She was perfection.

He kissed her in the light shade of the willow, and they came home, had dinner and went to bed, lying in each other's arms to the quiet sound of moorhens splashing in water. It was peaceful now he'd stopped the ploughshares and trumpets. Liberal minds didn't encourage that kind of thing, trying to make out that one person was more important than all the rest.

*     *     *

Sheriff Hezekiah Stern would have disagreed. He was not only the holder of the town's highest civic office, but also governor of the free school and the parish board, which meant he was in charge of orphans and vagrants. In his large powerful hands lay the option to grant, or else refuse, entry to the poorhouse and the house of correction. The last had of late years become less corrective than commercial. It somewhat resembled Pilar's orphanage, but without the certificates. Young girls in a state of penury were taken in, examined by Hezekiah, then turned over to his

33

sister, a lady known as Mrs Yeoman, to be trained in the way they should thereafter go. Now and again children were born if the girls had been in trouble, and thereafter the same thing happened, but took longer. It was never openly murmured that a large number of the children were the sheriff's own as a result of the initial examination, which took place in a room at the back.

Sheriff Stern had lately lost his appetite for orphans. He could by no means banish his persistent, nagging desire: the longed-for sight of the squire's lady naked. Having been provided with an upbringing devoid of graven images, he did not know what an angel looked like; but some folk-memory of the goddess Freya, seated at her wheel with her hair shining gold against the rising and the setting sun, stirred in his puritanical mind despite itself.

One day, by some means, he would have her; that was certain. A diet of browbeaten and terrified orphans should be replaced by a dish fit for a king, except that kings, by tradition, were not to be set up in any manner as better than anyone else. In such ways he agreed with her spindle-shanked husband, whom he could out-do between the sheets any night; but the trouble was to get between them in the first place. In a well-conducted town such as Leys, no scandal must arise that would affect his civic position. Otherwise, such a sight to be seen and savoured was worth waiting for; and he, Hezekiah Stern, was a man who from the beginning had always got what he wanted by the end. It was a sign of the Lord's favour to one of the elect.

In the meantime, his urges troubled him, but he still omitted to satisfy them by the usual means of a visit to the correction-house. It was more edifying to allow the lack of satisfaction to build up his inward being.

*       *       *

Sir Eldred's widow, who had not attended either his death-bed or his funeral, lived upstairs in a separate wing of the older part of the house, blind with syphilis caught from her husband in the days when they still cohabited. Of late years she had spent her days being read to, as Hannah the servant could read and write, and at the same time occupying herself with shredding old newspapers, once they were read to her, into stuffing to make pillows for the poor. Hannah had suggested it, being herself a correction-house orphan, by now in her late thirties. She had never been married, but as stated could read and write. She could also think, but seldom spoke. A servant didn't, unless addressed.

*       *       *

Stella had resolved to visit the dowager frequently, to try to bring some cheer into such a life. She and Gareth were so happy, loved each other so greatly, had so much joy and laughter to spare, that they could surely help so sad an old lady. It was worst of all that Lady Dorothy, who had been very well-born indeed, had failed in over twenty years of marriage to provide Sir Eldred with an heir, despite the reproach of copiously existing bootblacks, grooms, farm labourers and footmen. It was her, Stella's, own clear duty to make sure Gareth had a legitimate son as soon as possible, if only to overset the unpleasant old man's Will. It was improbable that the late Sir Eldred had had any real wish to help the townspeople, who seemed to be doing very well for themselves as it was. Stella had seen real poverty in the streets in Dublin, and there was none like that at Leys. Besides, they themselves needed the money to keep up the great house as it should be kept. Sooner or later, bills would begin to arrive. She hadn't stinted herself, and had enjoyed living as the county neighbours did: as had been hoped for at the Dublin seminary. Gareth hadn't prevented her.

She ascended the stairs, rose-coloured skirts held aside in one hand while the other held the steep narrow balusters. This was the old part of the house, built before comfort was thought of. She might be entering a different world;

even the air up here smelt musty.

She called out at the door, asking if she might enter; to knock, as she knew, was considered a sign of low breeding. If you were a duchess you swept in without apology. However a servant with a round face, in cap and apron, came and opened the closed door, curtsying and saying her ladyship was expected.

The room had a dim greenish light, as if under water, it might have been the effect of the thick summer trees outside, yet there was no summer here. The old woman sat bolt upright in her chair, her silver-headed stick beside her. She had once been handsome, with a reasonable fortune and a famous and ancient name. Now, there was nothing left. A living skeleton, the irises of its eyes inflamed behind dark spectacles, raised a head whose sparse white hair was contained in a goffered cap, by no means freshly laundered. Sir Eldred's widow didn't like things changed too often, just as she'd begun to feel almost comfortable.

'You will forgive my remaining seated to receive you,' grated the brittle voice of the very old. 'I do not walk readily now without aid. Nor can I see you clearly, though they tell me you have beauty if not breeding. Stand, I pray you, against the light, so that I can see your shape and if you look likely to bear a child.'

Flushing—she had resented two of the remarks—Stella went and stood against the window and its dim daylight. Below was the lake and its proud-necked swans. Swans waddled when they walked. An aristocrat was no better than anybody else unless something had been done to deserve the title. Papa had always said so, and Gareth agreed. Because this woman was blind, or nearly so, one mustn't answer other than civilly. She hadn't been asked to sit down. The room was empty of anything to stare at; a blind person found their way about more easily if there wasn't much in the way.

'I trust you are well,' she heard herself say uselessly. Such a being would never be well, had not been so for years, might as well be dead; but one mustn't think it. The sightless eyes might peer into her mind.

'I can see from the light that you have fair hair,' continued the dowager. 'So had I once. I was considered personable. As you can see to what I have come, remember that one day you yourself may be in like case. None of us know how we will end. Go now, and do not trouble me again. I have come to prefer solitude.'

She reached for her reticule and again began shredding paper into it, the thin torn particles falling down like grimy snowflakes. A gold wedding ring gleamed on her finger, otherwise she wore no jewels, not even a mourning brooch. Stella hoped that the exercise of her preferred charity passed her days faster than if she sat doing nothing. She herself curtsied, then left with a formal word of farewell.

On the way downstairs again she found that she was trembling. *One day you yourself may be in like case.* God forbid. She and Gareth were happy. She must forget this terrible visit, put it behind her. Certainly she would not attempt it again. She wondered how much the old woman knew, or guessed, of events; she'd evidently known something about oneself; lack of breeding, the wife of the young man who'd stopped the traditional beating of ploughshares. No doubt the maid—her name was Hannah, she'd heard—had acquaintance in the town, and would bring news into the chosen solitude.

Hannah the servant had watched her go. So beautiful, and Hezekiah Stern had determined to have her; she'd seen him watch her ladyship's arrival with lust in his cold eyes. That man got them all in the end; it would only be a matter of time. When Hannah herself had arrived at the correction-house fifteen years ago, her mother having died penniless, he'd laid her down wordlessly in the back room they'd used for interviews. She'd been a virgin, so escaped the subsequent ceremonial whipping if you weren't. Testing for a maidenhead was part of his appointment, at least they all supposed so. It wouldn't have mattered anyway in her own case, being sent into service with Sir Eldred shortly afterwards.

He'd got at her the first time when she was clearing ash out of the grate in the library. There had had to be other times, as you didn't answer back in service, but he'd never given her a baby or the pox, which was something. Looking after the old lady was taxing, but on the whole an improvement. There were at least no surprises.

Hannah thought again about the new young Lady Seaborne. She hoped fortune would be kind to her; she'd meant to be kind today herself, coming upstairs by arrangement. Kindness didn't signify at Leys, and never had. No doubt her young ladyship would learn as much quite soon.


## CHAPTER FIVE

At first, despite the dowager's rebuff and the stiff initial curiosity of visiting society, Stella was happy at Leys House. The late squire had in his youth gone on the Grand Tour, and had collected a number of beautiful and interesting objects in the way of statuary, furniture and silver. She made acquaintance with these, also rummaged in the attics for forgotten things, some of which needed repair by experts in London. All this kept her occupied while Gareth continued his inspection of the farms and his schemes for their improvement. He would return at dinnertime, full of talk about Middle Whites and milk yields and how too many fields had been allowed to lie fallow. 'A lot of it was his fault,' he would say, glancing up at the portrait of the late Sir Eldred in his claret-coloured coat, a colour which was too near that of his face to become him.

'Let's hang it somewhere else,' said Stella, adding that it was enough to put you off your breakfast. This had been the initial cause of discontentment of Mrs Stevens, who said the portrait had always hung there and should be left.

'It will go where my husband says it will,' replied Stella. In the end it was hung in the hall, to greet arrivals. Gareth said he would have a portrait of Stella in her blue gown painted instead, as it matched her eyes. The prospect consoled her; she was beginning to be discontented. The county here, she said, looked down their noses because she was Irish. She hadn't returned more calls.

Gareth knew he himself would have to go across to Raheere soon again. Dan O'Toole was doing well enough, but the tenants needed him, the industry founder, to encourage them and spur them on. He didn't want to leave Stella, but for her to travel back and forth across the rough tides from the Welsh coast would—he didn't like to say it to her—make an heir less likely. It was becoming urgent to secure the prospect of one; they'd been here eight months, making love constantly, and still no sign.

Mrs Stevens, in dudgeon in town, was meantime spreading stories about the extravagance of the new young lady of the manor. Her husband didn't keep an eye on her, that was well seen. Meantime, Mrs Stevens' son Jack, who found his task of keeping the carriages bright and shining, and ensuring that the wheels were oiled and didn't stick or fall off, more to his taste after all than standing about and getting varicose veins, drove her ladyship when Sir Gareth was away. Frequently they took the four-wheeler, as the maid Pilar, promoted to housekeeper, often accompanied her mistress in the way she had done in Dublin.

A return visit was forced on Stella at last by a personage named Mrs Abigail Comstock. Mrs Comstock greatly resembled a peahen, and was otherwise the kind of woman who sits on committees when there are any, and if there are not, will start one. She had called at Leys one day out of a wish to see the great house for herself—Sir Eldred hadn't encouraged her sort, and his wife entertained nobody—but also to ask Stella to lend her patronage to a contemplated charity for gathering in, by means of lay missions, the poverty-stricken saved, or such as were to be found.

Stella was uncertain what a lay mission

might be or who the saved were; such matters had not been among those discussed at her father's house as far as she knew. However she was anxious to make herself liked here among these sour-faced people if it was possible. 'The meetings will be held in the town hall on the first Tuesday of each month,' said Mrs Comstock, rising with a gratified shaking out of dun-coloured skirts; she really was very like a peahen indeed, and after she had gone off Stella went and watched the gloriously coloured male birds strutting and shaking their terra-cotta seasonal backsides, and all in search of a plain little mate.

When Gareth came home she told him what had transpired. 'Lord, you shouldn't have agreed, dearest,' he said. 'It's a sect not everybody belongs to. Some are saved and others are damned, and if you're damned there's no hope for you.'

'If they're saved anyway, why trouble to collect them at all?'

'They have to have a list for reading out the names at the Last Judgment. I should have warned you. Forgive me, but we must say you have other engagements and cannot after all attend.'

'That would cause ill-feeling. I do not want to do that.'

'As you please, then, my darling.' He always gave way, and kissed her to console her. What would have done so rather less was the

43

knowledge, which Stella did not have but Mrs Comstock did, that the sheriff was president of the new charity and had particularly suggested that young Lady Seaborne be invited.

She went to the meeting, and found Stern's physical nearness disturbing, but was uncertain why.

## CHAPTER SIX

Sheriff Hezekiah Stern, despite his propensities, was a man to whom solitude was at times essential. For this reason he had never taken unto himself a wife. Mrs Comstock, who was a widow, had for some time cherished the hope that the high sheriff might ask her to become the helpmeet of his bosom, but her hopes had by now turned to vinegar. She continued to attend his weekly extempore sermons at the sectarian chapel less for bitter-sweet communings than by reason of the fact that you got a good gossip afterwards and picked up all the news. This time, she was able to inform everybody that Lady Seaborne had agreed to become a member of the new charity committee.

'But is she saved?' was the cry. Abigail had to admit she didn't know; with the Irish, you could never be certain one way or the other.

The sheriff had suggested her ladyship, so it must be in order.

\* \* \*

Lacking a wife, Hezekiah's domestic needs were met by his only sister, who had succumbed in youth to the advances of an Australian sea-captain. His name was Yeoman, a proof that he was not of convict descent. This fact being accepted, his courtship of a member of the tight-lipped Stern family was tolerated. The marriage took place, and the new Mrs Yeoman set out with her spouse across seas. As everyone knows, the voyage takes a considerable time. By February, which is a very hot month in the Antipodes, the landing was accomplished, and a strange young woman hurled herself without warning or permission into Captain Yeoman's arms, followed by several children. In this way, the former Miss Stern learnt to her chagrin that she was merely a part of a whole; the gallant captain had a wife and children at Parramatta already.

In deep mortification, the betrayed spinster wrote home to her brother for the return fare, but by the time it arrived—he did send it off at once—she had given birth to guilty fruit in the shape of a small scrubby boy named Henry. He remained, for the sake of propriety, with the first Yeoman contingent, who were cheerfully

45

willing to have him provided money was regularly sent for his upkeep.

In this state of aridity, cured for all time of bodily passion, Mrs Yeoman, as she still called herself—the whole business was too difficult to explain—otherwise came home to Hezekiah. Being the man he was, Hezekiah proceeded to make use of the knowledge he possessed to acquire a lifelong, and unquestioning, slave. The spurious Mrs Yeoman, in perpetual terror of being unmasked, ran the house of correction for him exactly as he prescribed. No questions were asked, and nothing was witnessed or repeated. Only when orphans were sentenced to whipping did the matron, birch in hand, begin to resemble Clytemnestra or Medea, doing the job as thoroughly as she helped to falsify the books. When benevolently disposed persons came by arrangement to inspect, hire or donate, everything was perceived to be exactly as it ought. If pox, which Hezekiah was careful not to catch, was discovered in an inmate, she was douched with permanganate and marked down for employment to some master who conveniently had the disease already. The efficiency of the sheriff and his sister made it unlikely that they would be superseded in office in the lifetime of either. Nobody else really wanted the honour anyway, and the bringing up of mysteriously appearing babies in the way they ought to go, and their eventual apprenticeship, brought in a good revenue to balance the official books.

Like others, the Seabornes had made the requisite visit. Pilar was with them, everybody was given tea, shown the orphans at their sewing and laundering, then the carriage bowled home. Pilar was silent, but she never said much. Those places were the same wherever you went. The sheriff's sister might be as mim as you liked, but she'd be a proper tartar when nobody was watching. As for him, he was like something on a gravestone.

\*     \*     \*

Proximity to Stella on the charity-committee did not help Hezekiah; he was unable to make headway. Lady Seaborne was polite, but remained distant, evidently unmoved either by his godliness or his dark-clad masculinity. She declined an invitation to come and hear his sermons, and when he attempted to call at Leys to discuss some matter of collecting together the saved, was informed by Pilar that her ladyship was not receiving. This snub heightened Stern's unslaked desire remarkably; a diet of orphans became more than ever irrelevant. Lady Seaborne appeared to be given to somewhat frivolous pursuits; the sheriff decided to attend the annual subscription ball, as was not his habit. Tight-fisted and grudging every pennyworth of the

47

admission ticket, he stood, gloomy in blacks, to witness the ungodly dancing.

Gareth and Stella were on the floor, taking part in that most heathen institution, the waltz. They danced as one, he handsome in a blue coat and snowy stock, she in a dress with spangles. The sheriff rightly cogitated on the cost, at the same time surveying the cleft between Stella's white and comely breasts above the immodest neckline. Everybody knew the couple were spending money they had not yet got and which, in the circumstances, would soon by right be the townspeople's. As it was, the new carriage had the Leys monogram on the doors, and a fine pair of greys to draw it; and Sir Eldred having made a point of drinking all the wine before he died, Sir Gareth was known to have laid down a cellar. Also, there was a rumour that a great deal had been given to help the potato famine in Ireland at the request of her ladyship's father. The whole thing was misguided, to say the least.

They had in fact been hoping for a baby by the spring, and had run up bills accordingly. They were aware, as they waltzed, of the grim presence of the sheriff and of his cold eyes following. 'It's like having Oliver Cromwell watching us,' Stella whispered; in a small town everything you said was repeated if they heard. Her cheek was against Gareth's, and he turned and kissed her. The sheriff's disapproval was evident.

'No wonder they draw the curtains at Sidney Sussex before the Loyal Toast,' said Gareth in his accustomed voice. 'All the same, Old Noll's face wasn't as bad as all that. His wife was fond of him.'

'Wives are often fond of their husbands. I'm fond of mine.'

'As I am of you, Stella. Milton, now had a bad time with his first. Original sin took on the wrong face after he wrote *Paradise Lost*. If they'd got on better, his outlook would have been different. All the same I can forgive him for a great deal because of the lines about Sabrina.'

'Say them.'

The Dublin school hadn't included *Comus*. Gareth obliged.

*'Sabrina, fair,*
*Listen where thou art sitting*
*Under the glassy, cool, translucent wave.*

If we ever have a daughter, let's call her Sabrina.'

'We ought to have a son first. A daughter won't count in the stakes against these townsfolk. Look at them watching us now, trying to see if I'm going to have anything at all. I only wish it would happen, but it hasn't.'

'We must keep trying.' The music played on.

'I like trying, don't you?' said Stella. 'All the same it ought, by now—'

The waltz ended, and they twirled off the

49

floor. Stella felt guilty about the sheriff; she hadn't encouraged him, and there was no need to be uncivil now Gareth was with her. Still with the lack of any baby sadly in mind, they went to talk to the solitary figure in black. He bowed slightly. His hands itched to grasp Stella's body, almost to indulge with her in the ungodly dancing. That husband couldn't serve her; four years married, and no child! His own longing consumed him; at nights, in his solitary bed, his mouth would grow dry with longing, his parts racked with it. Now she was near him, propriety must overcome; but she was addressing him without the deference expected from a woman of his own kind.

'Why do you not dance, sir sheriff?' She hoped he wouldn't ask her, all the same.

'Because I regard it as a sinful pastime.'

'Then why come?'

She was pert, he decided; she needed a master. Unaware and smiling, she danced off again in the arms of her husband. The strains had started up once more and would continue, and he had no place here. After watching for a few more resentful moments he made his way out. Now that she was no longer present in his gaze it was easier to picture her in his bed. Those breasts, like young melons! They would fill both his hands. Her mouth, and her thighs, he would cause to open, despite her.

He decided that he would get into the habit

of taking a walk daily, early in the morning, down towards Leys House. Once he had the young squire's lady on her back, he could do as he would. She wouldn't say anything afterwards, for fear of scandal.

He passed a pale tongue across his lips, and saw their carriage bowl past. Their heads were still together, like young lovers. Four years with her in bed, and nothing to show! Envy and scorn consumed Sheriff Hezekiah. He knew himself a fit rival, given the opportunity.

\*    \*    \*

After he had left Stella said she was glad he'd gone. 'He reminds me of all the things St Paul said women weren't to do. They weren't to speak up in public, or get drunk.'

'Nobody at all was to fornicate, and I want to, with you. Let's go home.'

They had gone out hand-in-hand into the lavender night. The new carriage waiting, shining in the light of its hung lanterns. As they drove along they saw the dark figure of the sheriff still walking, head down, hat replaced squarely.

'He frightens me,' said Stella. 'I don't know why.'

She was trembling, and he put an arm round her. 'You're cold. You should have brought a shawl.' It was a warm night and they hadn't; that was it, no doubt.

51

Back at the house Pilar, who had been watching for their return, slept when at last they did. She could always hear them making love. Sir Gareth was happy: that was the main point.

## CHAPTER SEVEN

Daniel O'Toole surveyed the filled glass Gareth had poured him as if he ought not to be drinking it. He had witnessed the terrible aftermath of the recent potato famine in Ireland and had a clear memory of the faces of the starving. He had come over in person to ask for more money, of which Gareth had already sent generous sums to buy copper sulphate for the new leaves of next year's harvest. It was said to make the bristly-worm, that destroyed potatoes, less likely. 'If a country's left too poor to live on any kind of food but one, the one must be saved,' Dan said, without any sense of irony as to the application of the word here at Leys. Some of those better off, on the larger owned farms, had slaughtered chickens to make soup and had ladled it out to the starving people, especially the children. 'In England you have cheap bread,' Dan said. 'There they have nothing. For all the harm that has been done to them, there should be atonement. It would hearten them at Raheere if yourself was to come. They can't work when they're hungry.'

Gareth found the older man's dedication gnaw at him. The time was coming when he would have no more to give, unless Stella conceived a son; she'd been to London to see a doctor, who said there was nothing wrong. He murmured that he must stay at Leys for the next few weeks at any rate, and would come then. Dan was talking now about how they'd found that scraping soot from the insides of the chimneys helped the potatoes to grow without blight. 'The government should send aid,' he finished, and at last drained his glass.

Stella had been listening idly. Uncle Dan was a crusader, forever with some cause; he was like her father in that, but Brian O'Toole had himself been pouring out article after bitter article to be read both in Ireland and in England. He had made enemies among the Establishment, who didn't like to be disturbed, and Daniel said his brother had received threatening letters. It was a sad and unending business, and she herself could think of nothing but the recent visit to the London doctor. Nothing wrong; but still no child coming. Soon the townsfolk would claim their rights. What would happen then? Could they sell Leys House? She didn't know; and was for once aware of how little she knew anyway. She rose and left the dining-room, and the two men talking; as she reached the door she saw

Gareth reach for his cheque book. He couldn't afford to give any more money, for copper sulphate or anything else, but nothing would stop his generosity. She herself wouldn't like him to be mean.

She went into the drawing-room and began to strum tunelessly on a little Irish harp her father had given her when she was married. *The Harp that Once.* It was one tune she remembered; and the words. *But freedom now so seldom wakes.* Freedom was never encouraged; when it came to it, there had to be revolutions. She heard the badly-tuned notes of the little harp sounding flatly in the silence. The London doctor's voice came again in her mind. His consulting room had been in Wimpole Street. She'd taken Pilar. The doctor had appeared, pleasant and confident, had examined her and said there was nothing wrong. 'Perhaps your husband values you too much; he should be more forceful,' he had ended, smiling and adding that most women came for the opposite reason, they couldn't stop having 'em. There was a man called Towne in Lisson Grove who dealt with that sort of thing, as he himself, of course, didn't. He had bowed her out, wishing her better fortune and a fine son before long.

For some reason she remembered the name of Towne, and Lisson Grove. It was a place where young girls were taken when they were in trouble.

She moved restlessly, setting the harp aside. Perhaps after all she should entertain more company. Such as had already come did not appeal to her; there had been a woman the other day, one of the hunting fraternity, who remarked bluntly on Stella's lack of an heir and said she should take more exercise. 'Join the hunt, you and your husband,' she said, adding that her own two little angels were walking in the garden this minute with their nurse, and were being taught to ride early; it was best to start young.

'Neither my husband nor I like hunting,' Stella had replied firmly. 'We are sorry for the foxes, and still more the little harmless hares.'

The woman had looked at her as if she were mad, and had soon left. After she had gone Stella had thought angrily about what had been implied, both by the London doctor and the weather-beaten huntswoman. Gareth wasn't manly enough, forceful enough, too gentle and kind. She remembered how on their wedding night the quick pain, soon over, of his taking of her virginity had surprised and shocked him so greatly he wouldn't touch her again for some time. Such matters were put right now, but he still handled her like Dresden china. Within herself she knew, without admitting it, that there was a part of her he had never reached, much as she loved him and he her. She wanted to give him the whole of herself, bear his children, be a wife to him. Soon, Uncle Dan would drag him away again to Ireland. There must by then be hopes of a son, here at Leys: there must.

That night they made love. Next day Stella woke early and looked down at her sleeping husband. His head, the cinnamon hair ruffled, lay close against her, his arm flung across her still, as if in memory of their gentle delight together. He adored her and she him; what a darling he was, so handsome and clever, and her slave! He would do anything she asked.

He would do anything she asked.

It was perhaps then that the idea came to her. Because he didn't enjoy, any more than she did, the spectacle of a terrified animal being torn in pieces was nothing to do with it. They both loved animals. She remembered little Talley in Dublin, and how she had loved him; mercifully the end had been quick, not like that of the foxes and hares. She would never have another dog. There must, though, be a child. The tradesmen were beginning to press for payment and Sir Eldred's fortune, once gained, would pay for copper sulphate as well; that would quiet her conscience.

Yes, she'd thought of it. Pilar was like her right hand, and would do anything for her. She must persuade Gareth: that was the difficult part. The mention of the need in Ireland would convince him, surely, if nothing else did.

She kissed him, seeing his eyes open sleepily, like a little boy's. He turned towards

56

her and she felt him slip into her again, as if it was the most natural thing in the world. Outside, rain had begun to patter on the window. She hoped the hunt was getting thoroughly wet. There was no need to go out, no need to get up. Uncle Dan would have left early to catch the boat back, taking his cheque with him.

Lying together as they were, Stella began to outline her plan, keeping her arms tight about Gareth, her mouth against his own. That way, he had to listen. To be able to pay the tradesmen would, after all, be a roundabout way of benefiting the townsfolk. Later on, she'd talk to Pilar.

*  *  *

With Pilar, she brought in mention of the Bible, which had been used in instruction at the orphanage. Pilar knew already that the patriarchs' wives, Sarah and Rachel, while still unable to bear children of their own, had told their husbands to sleep with their maids, and the results had been born between the wives' knees. 'I wouldn't go as far, but I'll stuff pillows down myself when there's company, and look as if I'm going to have a baby,' Stella said. 'We'll keep you hidden towards the end. It can be done, I'm sure, if you will agree to this for us, Pilar. You know what it means to have the money.'

57

Pilar knew. She was beginning to have to fend off the tradesfolk, who by now were demanding payment before they would deliver. She looked down at her hands.

'There's one thing,' she said slowly. 'Sir Gareth won't find me a maid. My first master ruined me, but he didn't give me the pox. I'm healthy, as far as I know.'

Stella looked at the thin small wiry body, and smiled. 'You must lie in my bed for it,' she said. 'The other servants mustn't be given a chance to guess.'

She was the least concerned of the three. Gareth had been horrified. 'I couldn't be unfaithful to you,' he said. 'I love you.'

'Abraham loved Sarah and Jacob loved Rachel, and afterwards they got on all right. It's only for the time being, and for good reasons. You don't have to deal with these tradesmen. Pilar and I do, and with the county, and everyone. It's not asking much of you, my darling. It'll be dark, and you can pretend it's me.'

He had never, in the end, resisted her. He agreed, miserably. It was against his conscience, but the Will had been unjust. He would keep that in mind, and behave like Abraham, if he could. After all there were precedents.

\*     \*     \*

Pilar lay in the master bed and waited for Sir Gareth. She knew that this was the most important night of her life, and that if she could give birth to a son of his, the crown. Nobody had ever known how greatly she loved him, and now she would let him know without words. When she heard him come into bed, she turned to him: neither of them spoke.

Yet a spark was kindled, as it had been the day he met Stella. He had never know passion as strong in any woman, let alone quiet Pilar. It began to possess him totally. He forgot who he was, who she was, he the squire, she the servant and, for tonight, the concubine; he forgot why they were here together. There was only this hour in time, when her limbs enclosed his own so fiercely that an embrace took place the like of which, in his whole conventional life, he had never dreamed could exist; the unleashed, inherited passion of the old Visigoths of early Spain. A drop of it was in her blood from her mother, and for the night it came into its own; he felt his seed run into her freely, a hot uncontrollable stream. By dawn, dazed, he turned to find she had left him and gone to her own place. He sought out Stella, and sat for a long time with his face against her snowy neck. 'I pretended it was you,' he said. He knew he was lying. For the first time since they met, he had forgotten her. The memory itself began to embarrass him.

He said he couldn't face Pilar again quite

yet, and would go to Dan at Raheere. Stella tried to dissuade him. 'Once may not be enough,' she said.

'You can send me word.' He was afraid of it happening again. 'Oh, Stella, Stella, I love only you; do you believe it?'

'Think of being able to pay the tradesmen, and sending the copper sulphate, as much as they need.' She must turn his mind to other things. It needn't happen again after all, unless it must. For the time, he was no doubt better away.

*     *     *

Three weeks later Pilar came to her and said it was all right, it had worked. Her small face betrayed no emotion. Within herself she could always hug the memory of that one night with his arms holding her, her limbs entwined in his, the feeling of his heart beating against hers, the pair of them made one. It would never happen again, but she would bear his child. Hagar had been cast out by Abraham into the desert afterwards, but she wouldn't be. Miss Stella was pleased, and said she'd start stuffing herself with pillows.

# CHAPTER EIGHT

Stella had sent in her resignation from the charity-committee, saying that she was in a certain situation. She also had herself driven through town wearing the first pillow. It wasn't so comfortable that she would risk walking with it. However, with one thing and the other the news spread like wildfire that her ladyship really was, at last, in the family way. Those who had laid their bets otherwise at the inns sadly expected to have to pay up.

Among the first to call to congratulate Stella was the insufferable huntswoman, herself expecting a third by dint of approved exercise. 'Our darlings will be able to grow up together,' she announced. Stella smiled and said nothing. The woman was a climber, and she had already learned to beware of such at Leys. To be on nodding terms with the squire's lady was considered something, even though they didn't go out with the pack.

Worse by far was the formal visit of Sheriff Hezekiah, both to regret her resignation and to congratulate her on its cause. Stella had no means of knowing the fierce resentment that consumed him, nor did he make it evident. He stood like a colossus, his thick powerful thighs, clad in their dark broadcloth, straddling the delicate needlepoint hearthrug of the smaller drawing-room where she lay, suitably padded, on the sofa. She had the impression that the cold eyes penetrated her bodice, the padding, and beneath that her very nakedness, as if it were revealed. This, as she now knew, was the reason for her constant discomfort at his nearness during meetings in the town hall. It occurred to her that a night spent in bed with such a man would leave one like a wrung rag. After he had gone her knees felt weak, and she gave orders to the servants—Pilar was resting upstairs—that for the present she would receive no further callers.

Nevertheless she went up, later on, to see how Pilar fared. It was important that the early months should be undisturbed. Gareth was in Ireland, and she had only his loving letters to rely on. Her father was well, and busy with his articles. Laracor Industries were reviving in the wake of the famine. *It must never be allowed to recur,* Gareth wrote. He didn't ask about Pilar. It was as though that had never happened. Stella remembered the huntswoman's advice about exercise. Pilar mustn't sit about all day, knitting and mending; it wasn't that she was idle. She still looked the same as usual, perhaps a trifle thicker about the waist.

'We must go for walks in the early morning,' Stella told her. 'As time passes it will be the only hour of the day when nobody is about. I can't bear these pillows for nine whole months.

We can wear our Laracor cloaks.'

They began to do this, and a third person necessarily to be let into the secret was Hannah. She was discreet, had no wish to see the townspeople gain, least of all the sheriff; also, it would be needful to have her help at the time of the birth.

They began, therefore, to take these early walks, and the fresh air was as welcome as the peace. Stella would get up at dawn to rouse Pilar, glad of the excuse not to stuff pillows down herself till later on. She had by now added a second and a third for afternoons, in case of callers; although forbidden, you never knew for certain. Stella began to understand how Pilar must be beginning to feel, with her small body by now so distended she couldn't see her feet when she walked. Both of them wore their Laracor cloaks, for concealment whatever the weather.

On a particular morning a wind arose. They had walked past the waterfowl and the peacocks, and had gained the field beyond. 'Is it too far for you?' Stella asked Pilar; one must be careful of her by now.

'No, my lady.'

The gale blew, but no rain with it; to walk was welcome. Stella walked as slowly as she might, though her young body longed for a more vigorous challenge. The wind blew about her cloak and gown, outlining her strong shapely thighs, slim waist and flat abdomen beneath the glorious breasts. Beside her, Pilar was a little round stuffed dumpling. The wind blew back her cloak also, and her advanced state was no longer hidden.

Nor was it unobserved. The sheriff was standing in the field near the hedge. His cold gaze surveyed both women. There was no doubt he'd seen. Stella confronted him, while Pilar pulled her cloak about herself, too late.

'What are you doing here? These grounds are private.'

She was like an angry Nordic goddess, hair blowing gold. He bowed, and said he had merely been taking a turn in the early morning as he often did.

'It is one of the few private times of the day, as no doubt your ladyship is aware,' he said. His gaze slid from Stella to Pilar, and back. Stella longed to slap his face. She wondered how often he'd been down here. He was not a huntsman and couldn't be after foxes. What did he want? What would he do, now he'd seen? She had been a fool to come here at all, out beyond the garden with Pilar looking as she did by this time.

She turned away, gesturing to Pilar to accompany her. 'Don't hasten,' she said. Haste might be dangerous, but it was not more so than the situation had become. However he would use it, the sheriff had them in his power.

She spent the next few days in trepidation, but nothing happened, except that Pilar went into labour at the expected time. In all ways, she was doing her duty.

*     *     *

It had been arranged with Hannah that as soon as the birth was over, Stella should take the baby and lie in bed with it, while Pilar recovered in private. Word would meantime be sent out that the squire's lady was in her throes. Stella had had nightmares including the old thundering of ploughshares, which incredibly might once have taken place at the news. The matter was one of deadly earnest. Gareth and she needed the money. The townspeople did not.

Meantime, she could not be anywhere but with Pilar, who was biting her lips valiantly. Soon she turned her head aside and hid her face, saying the child was coming. Hannah took it at last, twisting it out of her. It was a boy with darkened cinnamon hair. He was healthy and yelling. When he was dried and his nose and mouth cleansed, it could be seen that he was the image of Gareth.

Stella took him quickly and got into bed. Hannah would see to Pilar, who had made very little fuss. Stella sent a telegram off to Gareth. *You have a fine son.*

Bells had begun to ring already up in the town. It was being said already that the squire's son was like his father. Hannah had told Stevens, and Stevens' mother had told the world.

Stella began to breathe again. The sheriff had evidently held his peace. A feeling of unease, however, stayed with her.

## CHAPTER NINE

It was not until the day after the birth that Pilar's feelings towards Stella began to change. When this happened it was swift, deadly and irrevocable.

She did not see Gareth set eyes on his son, though he came home at news of the birth, arriving very early the day after. Hannah brought words that he was very pleased and was going to make Pilar a gift of money. She didn't want the money. She had borne a son to the man she loved, and her small breasts had begun to fill with milk. She waited for them to bring back the baby, to feel his hands pushing at her, his mouth pulling at her, taking sustenance as puppies and kittens did. At such times, he would be hers and nobody else's. Otherwise, Hannah said his father had put his name down for Eton. That was the business of others; feeding him was hers. She was cold with anxiety when Hannah came to her at last with a length of linen, and began to bind up her breasts.

66

'That'll put you right again, dear. My word, you've done well. No need to bother about feeding. Sir Gareth arranged for a wet-nurse some time ago, otherwise her ladyship says people would wonder why she's kept her figure. It's that goes for it, rather than the birth. You'll get yours back.' She finished binding up the linen band, and fastened it with an expert knot. 'It's feeding spoils it, not the labour. You're to have a good rest, my lady says, and not be seen about again until you're ready.'

So her baby had been taken away altogether. She wasn't even to feed him. She was to be given money for having obliged, then permitted to watch a young stranger grow up and be sent to Eton. He was never to be allowed to mean anything to her, or she to him, or else people might talk.

Well, that had been the arrangement, no doubt; she hadn't taken in the cruelty of it till now. Sir Gareth would come home now and again and he and her ladyship would make love night after night, the way they'd always done, and without his ever giving as much as he'd given to herself; and he didn't want to remember. He hadn't come to see her after the birth, even for moments; he'd been kept away. Twice altogether, when she was expecting, he'd come home, had been formal and distant, the master with the servant, as if nothing had ever happened between them. No doubt it was the correct thing to do; he might even put it out of his mind now he and Miss Stella had their heir. Well, she, Pilar, hadn't forgotten. She would keep the memory of that fierce night of triumph in her mind, in her heart, for as long as she lived. Whatever else they had taken away, they could never take that; and they would never know, from looking at her face, what she felt about that or anything.

\*         \*         \*

Time passed. She would see the baby at times in the distance, carried by his nurse. Then there arrived a second nurse, who slept in his room and saw to him, and later began to teach him to walk. Sir Gareth and her ladyship didn't have too much to do with him, being wrapped up in each other as always. As for the money, it was safe now; there was an heir. The bills were paid. She'd done her duty.

One day they heard the wheels of an arrival. It proved to be Daniel O'Toole, his face ashen. She heard him go into the downstairs room and before the door closed say, 'You'll not have heard?'

It was soon enough in the papers, but before then Sir Gareth had gone back with O'Toole to Ireland for his father-in-law's funeral. It hadn't been an accidental death. It had been murder, whatever anyone said. At the funeral hundreds of poor folk followed the coffin, in silence except for the sound of their moving shuffling feet.

'You could have done nothing,' Dan O'Toole had said, when Gareth reproached himself for not being there. 'How could you have foreseen it? None of us did, and we knew the feeling there was. The Establishment, the rich absentee landlords, didn't like Brian. He was bringing the rights of the poor before the public, and that made those who weren't poor uncomfortable.' He put back a lock of thick hair, white now, from where it had fallen over his eyes, and went on. 'He was walking in the street, late it was, after the office had closed for the day, taking the air for a while as he did always. A man of my Lord Boteler's, who's hot for the Establishment and has several times tried to close the paper down, shoved him into the road just as my lord's own carriage came by. It was a concerted thing, no accident. The carriage drove over him not once but three times, driving back and forth till he was crushed. My lord said afterwards he had turned the carriage to find out what the commotion was. He—my brother—couldn't have been alive by the time we could get to him. It's been hushed up, of course. I came myself, for that reason.'

'Who will run the paper, now?' Gareth asked. He knew it was the kind of question his father-in-law would have wanted; the dead were dead, the crushed corpse buried with honour. Brian O'Toole would not be forgotten in Ireland.

'We was wondering if yourself would come until we find someone. You know what's wanted and how he would have written it. You wouldn't let the paper die.'

Stella had wept for her father, but didn't want to go back to Dublin. 'Come when you can,' she said. 'I will be well enough looked after.'

It was impossible to think of Papa as dead. They'd called the boy Brian Laracor after him. It must have been a premonition. She would stay here with him, and the life here. It was her duty, safer and more comfortable.

Daniel and Gareth had ridden off, and the town was told that her ladyship's father had died suddenly in Ireland and that the squire would not be home again for some time. Nobody at Leys knew much more, except the high sheriff. Hezekiah Stern was always informed of events as soon as possible. He did not pay a visit of condolence, remembering his earlier snub. Instead, he had other plans.

\*     \*     \*

Stella, on her official recovery from the birth, began to throw herself into the part of squire's lady even though the squire himself was elsewhere. It was necessary to keep up appearances, and her clothes had never been of the latest mode over here. She had herself conveyed to town, and ordered a great many new dresses, hats with feathers, muffs for the winter, calfskin shoes and gloves not made by Laracor. It wasn't that she had anything against the enterprise, and wished dear Gareth well; but she herself was striving to become an Englishwoman, mother of an English heir to an English title. She began to return calls, although she still wouldn't hunt.

Only once or twice, when she looked in the glass and saw her own glowing reflection, did Stella remind herself that the whole thing was a lie, because of the old squire's money. Perhaps his ghost would come back to haunt her. Nevertheless some of the money had done a great deal of good to the poor people of Ireland, so she could surely afford to be somewhat frivolous here, across the water.


CHAPTER TEN

Pilar was returning late one morning with a basket full of brown eggs over her arm. The home farm kept one or two hens Miss Stella especially favoured, and by now she, Pilar, being as it were one of the family—her mouth twisted a little—could take one or two for her own breakfast; they were so fresh the whites

71

were still curdled. Small pleasures were, after all, something.

She was accosted by the rat-faced Stevens, and asked rather sharply what he wanted. 'It's not me as wants yer, it's the sheriff,' he answered, his eyes full of the lack of interest any woman aroused who was as plain as Pilar. 'I'm to drive yer up.'

'Well, I'm not taking the eggs with me,' Pilar replied briskly, and vanished into the kitchen quarters with instructions to take some upstairs. She reappeared in her cloak.

They drove off, and to the clopping of the hooves she wondered what the sheriff wanted. It wasn't likely to be anything pleasant. She must keep her wits.

She was shown into the inner hall, where Stern sat at his high desk on a platform, writing with a quill. He took some moments to raise his head, and she was left standing. Presently he laid down the quill. The cold eyes assessed her.

'If I order you to be stripped naked now, my good woman, there is evidence that you have borne a child out of wedlock; certain marks on the abdomen persist. I doubt if such marks are to be found on the fair body of your employer, young Lady Seaborne. In your own case, I can order you by statute to be whipped thrice round the town square till your shoulders bleed. What could be decided for defrauding the town's citizens of their due legacy might reflect harshly on yourself, on Lady Seaborne, and on her husband and his so-called liberal newspaper in Ireland. Do I make myself clear?'

She had felt the ground whirl under her feet, but she wouldn't oblige the bastard by showing fear. It wasn't fear for herself; she'd been whipped often enough, at the orphanage. Her son, the son she'd borne Sir Gareth, wouldn't inherit, and there would be nothing left anyway. Sir Gareth himself mustn't suffer; as regarding that, Pilar was determined. She would become supple as an eel if it was needed. She'd do anything, or almost anything. This sneering great brute in dark clothes, thinking he was God, shouldn't win by anything she did, or failed to do.

She said nothing, and waited. Sooner or later she'd learn from him why he'd sent for her. If all he wanted was to have her whipped at the cart's tail, he'd have ordered it. There must be something he wanted. If she waited in silence, by the end he'd say what.

Presently, he said it. She heard herself listen and answer. Yes, she'd do it. Yes, she'd see to everything. After that—her mind was as clear as water—she'd be in a position to take his precious reputation away from him, lose him his position, if she spoke out. He knew it; there was no need for promises. Now she'd agreed, they were equals.

Her small face was expressionless as she

went out and back to the carriage. She wouldn't give that Stevens the satisfaction of knowing what it was she'd been sent for to hear. She kept her hand tightly clasped in her lap on the drive home. It would be necessary to see Miss Stella at once. This was the only time she herself had left to think.

*   *   *

Stella had wept till her face was swollen, and sat now tearing at the fine stuff of her soaked handkerchief till it shredded like the dowager's newspapers. She'd been so happy, with the tradesmen paid and the baby in his cradle, and the shares transferred to Gareth's bank. The thing to do with a blackmailer was to expose him—they'd even been taught that at her polite Dublin school—but exposing Stern would mean having Pilar whipped, herself disgraced, Gareth made bankrupt, and the baby's future ruined. What was to be done? Stella began to batter her fists against her gown. His demand had been that he spend a night with her, in her bed here, before her husband's return. In exchange for that, he would keep silence.

She realised that Pilar had ordered tea; they often took it together when there was no company. Pilar set the laden tray down on the rosewood occasional table. As usual, she kept silence. Stella turned a woebegone face to her.

'Oh, Pilar, what am I to do? I cannot endure the thought of what he asks. I loathe him. I'm afraid of him.' She began to cry again.

'There is no other way,' said Pilar expressionlessly. 'It is only once, after all. He has promised it.'

'Once is too often. I could never endure it. I do not think I can agree. Gareth—'

'This will save him.' From bankruptcy; from parting with the great house here and their son's inheritance; Miss Stella's outward reputation and her position in society, which she cherished increasingly; all of that, and more. 'It is your duty to save your husband,' said Pilar sharply. 'To leave him without money and without hope, and in debt largely by your own doing, is sinful.'

She had never spoken so before in her life. Stella had slopped her tea over and the tears were dripping uselessly on her gown, which was new.

'You will ruin the silk,' said Pilar, and offered a clean corner of her apron. She felt nothing, not even triumph. The future of everything must not be put at risk because of one shallow young woman. Let her allow the sheriff a night's sated lust; that would be the end of it. 'Blow your nose, dry your eyes and think clearly,' she said, as though addressing a child; in ways, she thought, Miss Stella still was one. 'You can forget it afterwards; he doesn't have the pox, and once he has what he wants he'll not trouble you again. Otherwise, what is left?'

'My husband's love. I would not betray him.' Stella sniffed, and blew her nose on the remains of the handkerchief.

'You are spoiling his whole life if you will not do this one thing.' Pilar continued inexorably. 'His love for you may well fail in the end if you have brought him to beggary. You may end like the dowager upstairs, alone always, remembering only failure.'

'Oh, Pilar, save me from that. Nothing could be worse than that.' She thought of the blind dowager, with her dreadfully inflamed eyes. To end so!

'Save yourself. Nobody else can. You know what to do. I'll let him in.'

She herself saw the note despatched to the sheriff. It could have been read by anyone, and merely appointed a certain night, the one after tomorrow.

She still felt nothing. What must be done had to be. The rights and wrongs didn't matter. Sir Gareth, and her son, did.

*     *     *

Afterwards she went and stared, unusually, at her own reflection in Miss Stella's looking-glass. She saw a plain thin woman; had she expected to see a devil? Did she feel triumph already, at the prospect of Miss Stella's usage as a whore? Was the protection of her own lover of a night, and of their child, the least of it?

Perhaps nobody knew themselves for what they really were. It was best not to think of it, and get on with what must be done. There was no way out now, for any of them. Pilar dusted the glass absently, and went away.

## CHAPTER ELEVEN

Two nights later, Stella was brushing out her own hair before plaiting it. She had a maid to look after her clothes, but had dismissed her till tomorrow. The nurse next door had also been told that she might go home till the following morning.

Stella always brushed her own hair in the absence of Gareth. When he was here he liked to do it for her, a hundred strokes each side, loving the thick soft shining golden veil, delighting in its scented richness, burying his face in it. Now, it passed the waiting time to brush, and brush. Her fingers were trembling, and several times the ivory handle slipped from her hand. She would pick up the brush and start again. She didn't want to go to bed, and wait there till he came in. When it happened, she would close her eyes and pretend it was Gareth.

Gareth. She mustn't, after all, think of him now, or of the way in which she was having to betray him. What was to come was for his sake, as Pilar had said, but was also her own fault; she'd been extravagant. Otherwise, there might have been enough money to live carefully, but she'd liked being the squire's lady; new carriages, an extra footman to stand behind, new clothes, new curtains from London, an India rug and shawl.

A shadow moved. Stern had come into the room silently; she'd expected to hear his footsteps on the stairs. The brush fell from Stella's hand finally and clattered to the floor, as he came closer. He was so large he filled the room; there might have been nobody and nothing else in it. The thought came to her that her hair was still loose, and would tangle by the morning. Why think of that now?

She'd put on her prettiest bed-gown and nightgown, embroidered in Ireland by the Carmelite nuns. They made money over such things for food, otherwise had to leave a bowl outside the gate if they were starving. Think of that, think of her hair as it would be tomorrow. She rose to her feet, confronting the man who had come, the cold-eyed man without pity.

'Strip,' he ordered. When she hesitated he tore the bed-gown off by its sleeves, throwing it aside. He seized the nightgown and ripped it so that it fell to Stella's feet, leaving her naked. The eyes, as always, assessed her, concealing their amazement. He had never in his life seen such beauty, such perfection in a woman's body. What he had expected to see, had anticipated for long, was by far surpassed. This was the goddess of love. He recalled that she was mortal, that he must master her, and smacked her buttocks in a familiar way twice, then lifted her on to the bed. The counterpane was of lace, and must have cost something. He gazed down at the picture the squire's lady made, once more passing his tongue between his lips.

'Turn out the lamp,' she begged, but he might not have heard her. He stayed feasting his eyes for instants, then removed his shoes and climbed upon her. She had closed her eyes, and felt the thick desirous hands begin to pry and probe. After certain preliminaries, he entered her.

\*　　　\*　　　\*

Outside it was quiet; even the waterfowl were in their nests. Pilar, next door, had been rocking the empty pearwood cradle with her foot. She was possessed by bitterness. The nurse was to go home, and she had looked forward for once to her son's company even if he was asleep; but the woman had taken him with her. No doubt she'd been told to. She, Pilar, was to have no close connection with the squire's baby, no acquaintance beyond that of

79

a servant among servants. To rock an empty cradle was as much as they permitted her. She listened to the faint sound the rocking made, then became aware of another in the silence; the rhythmical creaking of the bed next door. He must have come in by the side entry she'd left unlocked by arrangement. He had been discreet and quiet on arrival: that was to be expected. Now, he was busy at what he'd come for. Her ladyship was being brought down to earth. Pilar knew, again, a devil's triumph. A second sound had begun to come through the wall and closed door; a man's avid gruntings. He'd be at her all night. Pilar reached for her knitting from her apron-bag and began to knit, silently and with grim endurance. The creaking would continue for a long time, then stop, then shortly begin again. The sheriff was taking his money's worth. Pilar's needles clacked quietly on. Somewhere in the distance a peacock waked in the darkness, and gave its harsh scream.

Towards dawn Pilar stole downstairs and set light to the fire laid ready beneath the copper boiler in the kitchen. My lady wouldn't be her usual self by morning, and would want a warm hip-bath. She, the good servant, would have it ready. Meantime there was no reason not to try to sleep. She undressed and slid into bed; it was not yet light. Out of the window Venus, pear-shaped, still hovered, luminous and low, in the sky.

Hannah also had been up most of the night, attending to some whim or other of her blind mistress. The old lady could be exacting, and Hannah had long grown into the habit of dozing off during the day, ready to wake if called in the intervals when the shredding of the newspapers, that had been read from aloud, was finished. Looking out of the window at the growing light, she could see, dimly, a man's figure making its way out of the side entrance of the house and across the gardens to the wicket gate. The jaunty set of his shoulders, his confident stride, were those of full physical satisfaction. Hannah spat. He wouldn't come down all this way for a maidservant. It must be her young ladyship. Hannah nodded to herself without surprise. The sheriff had ways of getting what he wanted, and he'd wanted my lady from the first hour he set eyes on her coming out of the carriage on the new squire's arm, with the ploughshares banging and the trumpets sounding as they'd used to. He'd waited till now. He was like a great spider, sitting in the middle of his web. She hoped that was the end of it, and that he wouldn't continue to trouble her ladyship whenever Sir Gareth was away.

\*      \*      \*

'Last night I heard fornication,' said the dowager later in the morning. 'It went on for a

81

long time. I know the sounds well enough from when my late husband was with the housemaids, but he seldom stayed as long. My hearing has become acute since I was made blind.'

'It might have been the new footman and his wife, my lady,' said Hannah soothingly. The man was married and his wife saw to the laundry.

'I doubt it. Footmen of necessity stand all day. They have not the resource left at the end of it to behave in such a way all night. Find out who it was. I do not sleep well, and would prefer not to be disturbed more than necessary.'

Hannah said she would try. It was the only answer.

\*     \*     \*

Later in the morning Pilar went into her mistress, finding Stella limp, exhausted and heavy-eyed with lack of sleep. She seemed ready to weep for shame. Her hair was tangled like a maenad's, the lace cover rumpled beyond belief. She had flung the bed-gown over herself, but the nightgown lay torn on the floor. Pilar picked it up.

'You will have to mend it,' Stella said. 'Get me a glass of salt water. I want to rinse my mouth out. Ugh. He put his tongue in it.'

'I've drawn a warm bath, my lady,' was all

Pilar said.

Shortly she helped Stella into the bath, bruises already darkening on the white arms and elsewhere. She seemed unable to stand at first, and staggered a little, then righted herself. A rim of foam was drying between her legs; Pilar noticed it. He hadn't been careful. If my lady had any sense, she'd get her husband home soon or else go across to him. You never knew.

\*       \*       \*

Shortly Stella wrote to Gareth in Ireland. She was beginning to feel queasy, and was greatly afraid.

> *My darling,*
> *I am beginning to feel the lack of you so much that I am ill. The days pass slowly and there's no news to tell. If you could only come over to comfort me a little I would welcome you with all my heart, but I know you are greatly occupied with the paper. Otherwise might I come to you, even for a few days? It seems a long time since I was in your arms.*
> *Your loving wife,*
> *Stella Seaborne*

She was so often sick now in the mornings that Pilar knew, but nobody else so far. It was Pilar who'd suggested she go over. 'He hasn't been home for weeks now, the squire, and if it has to be done we can say it's a seven-month birth,' was how Pilar had put it. Stella herself loathed her own body. At nights she would lie writhing, recalling his vast, determined parts thrusting up her to places she hadn't known she possessed. She must stop thinking about it. She must entertain company, otherwise there would be talk. Once, driven into town, she had encountered the sheriff, and stared coldly with her blue eyes as if she had never seen him before. His own had been altered very slightly from the usual, filled with cold triumph and the remembrance of his mastery of her, total and intimate knowledge of her flesh. She had almost fainted in the carriage, and hadn't gone into town again. A visit to Gareth was becoming necessary, though to deceive him made her feel worse than ever. As for her colour, it had faded; for the first time in her life she had to wear rouge, or there might, again, have been talk.

## CHAPTER TWELVE

Gareth wrote that he could not come meantime, but could spare a few days with her near the port if she would venture the crossing. She did so thankfully, driven by Stevens with Pilar there to see her off; but Stella made the journey alone, her veil drawn down. However the tides that day were rough, and she had to put the veil up now and again to be woefully sick. In the ordinary way it might have lost her the baby, and she wouldn't have minded; but how to greet Gareth bleeding from a miscarriage? It didn't happen, but she was pale and distressed enough on arrival to give likelihood to having been ill for lack of him. How deceitful she was becoming! The sight of him, with the sun, having struggled through, shining on his hair, cheered Stella, however, and he took her in his arms, which was even better.

'My darling, you are quite pale; what a terrible crossing it must have been! It's as well we do not have to travel on to Dublin.' He had taken a little cottage nearby for a few days, and even if he had to leave her sometimes to travel to town on business, he would be back by night.

The cottage was whitewashed and clean, and belonged to a farmer's widow who was an excellent cook and housekeeper. One of her daughters brought in their breakfast next day. By then they had made love often, in a fresh soft bed smelling of lavender. Stella felt the sins of the past melt away; he'd hesitated about taking her, saying she hadn't been well. 'I want you, I want you,' she had said truly, and in the end it had been as always between them.

During the day he would ride off to Dublin,

and Stella took her meals at the old farmhouse, with its roaring fires and old handcrafted furniture. The land had been farmed since Huguenot days, but several of the sons had gone abroad during the famines, to Australia and Canada. One was left, and had sons himself: but his mother and sisters were thinking of going to Dublin to set up a temperance hotel. That was how Gareth had got in touch with them, as they wanted to advertise in the paper, at first.

On Sundays Gareth was free all day, and he and Stella would walk out together arm-in-arm. They found fields with primroses, and a friendly donkey, Jacob sheep contentedly settled in their field, and black-and-white cows grazing. 'It's peaceful,' Gareth admitted, lying on the grass with his head on Stella's lap. He felt a tear fall on his face, and looked up.

'Dear love, why are you crying?'

How could she bear to tell him the truth? 'Because,' she said, 'we cannot always be together like this. I wish you were oftener at home.' That, at least, was true.

'It is not yet the best of all possible worlds, my darling, and won't be till I have found an editor, maybe not then. Anyone who can help this country should do so.' He wiped her tears dry, kissed her hand and held it. A gaggle of geese strayed past in the near distance, honking. 'Not everywhere is like this,' Gareth said. 'Even here the sons have left home to seek their fortunes abroad. There is still poverty, injustice and inequality. You know what befell your father.'

'Leave Uncle Dan to get on with it. You say he's getting tedious to live with. Come home.' He had already admitted that Daniel O'Toole, like many old bachelors, was growing difficult, set in his ways.

'I will move into Mrs Duveen's temperance hotel as soon as it's set up,' Gareth said firmly. 'She says there will always be a place there for me.'

Stella became a little jealous of Mrs Duveen, the tall handsome widow of Anglo-Norman descent who had long ago married the most eligible farmer in the county. The years had turned him into a bitter-mouthed old martinet before he died, and no doubt his women would be glad of their independence in Dublin. Stella began to resent Dublin, the *Tribune,* Raheere and the industry and the pending hotel. All of them kept Gareth away from her and from Leys, which, after all, he'd inherited and could spend now, if he would only do so, the leisurely life of a squire of English acres. This birth to come, which she mustn't mention, must certainly happen at Leys. If only he could be with her for it! As it was, deceitfully, she would have to write in a few weeks to say a child was expected. He must be led to think it had been conceived here. It wasn't his, any more than Brian

Laracor, as they'd called him, was hers. What a tangled state of affairs there was! She'd ceased to blame herself. It was somebody's fault, but not hers. That made it easier to bear.

\* \* \*

Gareth saw her off at the port, after their few days together. The tides would be better on the return voyage; it usually happened that way. The carriage would be waiting for her at the Pembroke side, with Stevens and Pilar. Increasingly, Stella began to feel that her husband's life and her own were becoming separate, that apart from the night she tried not to remember, when this coming child had been forced into her, Gareth already had interests which increasingly shut her out. It did not occur to Stella to try to share them; she wasn't made that way, Papa had never let her have anything to do with the paper or the cause, or anything but being brought up as a fine lady.

On the voyage back, she tried to remember the primroses. You didn't see them as thick in England any more.

\* \* \*

Gareth contrived to find a temporary editor within a month or two, and Mrs Duveen, having by then put him up and fed him well, promised, despite the stream of custom, to keep his room till he returned. Editions of the *Tribune* arrived weekly, a day or two late, at Leys. Stella by then had thickened, and lay mostly on a sofa. She had grown tearful when he couldn't be with her. He'd written that he was pleased about the child.

Brian Laracor had learned to walk, and Gareth, who had determined early to teach him to ride, sent orders for a small Shetland pony. Stella didn't pretend interest; she showed little affection for the child, but he seemed not to need it and was cheerful, a healthy and unremarkable little boy.

Pilar managed the house quietly, effacing herself. If Miss Stella went on thickening as fast, it was prudent to discourage visitors. Sir Gareth wouldn't know or suspect anything. He wasn't inclined in such ways, but the likes of that Mrs Comstock might notice, or the huntswoman. In that case she'd already suggested to Stella to say it might perhaps be twins. One couldn't be too careful. When labour started, it must be said to be at seven months. Nobody would be allowed to know the difference. Pilar knew she wasn't guarding Miss Stella in such matters, but Sir Gareth. On no account must he be hurt or dismayed.

# CHAPTER THIRTEEN

Stella's labour began nine months to the day after the sheriff had spent the night with her. Pilar, primed ready, sent a telegram to Gareth to say her ladyship had had a fall and the pains were coming early. Being a man, he wouldn't know, she thought, that premature babies sometimes didn't have hair or nails.

By the time he hurried across, the child had not yet manifested itself. Stella had laboured for twenty hours. Sheriff Hezekiah had planted his seed firm and high; she was rigid with fear lest what was about to be born should resemble him. 'Bear down, my lady,' Pilar kept saying, and when Gareth arrived he held Stella in his arms while she strove in vain, golden hair dank with sweat. She was afraid. 'Bear down.' She didn't want to, and resisted the force which was making its way inexorably out of her. She loathed the child. She loathed the memory. She only wanted Gareth's arms, his cheek against hers. It was all she wanted, and yet she was no longer in control of herself, there was another being forceful and active inside her. It had been moving a long time; but not like this. She'd never imagined such pain.

'Bear down.'

Why did they keep saying it? She didn't want to. She wanted to be left alone, with

Gareth, the way things had always been between them. This tearing force was something separate, alien, unknown. Stella began to howl, like a tortured animal, the tears streaming down her face.

It still wouldn't come. It must be placed crosswise, Hannah said. She was there, and in the midst of all of it Gareth decided that he didn't want Pilar present at the birth. He asked for her to be taken away. The whole household, and the town, he was told, were praying for her ladyship's safe delivery. When he told Stella this she began sobbing. 'I don't want it,' she kept saying. 'I don't want it.'

'There will never be others, darling, I promise.' It was his fault she was in this cruel state; he blamed himself, they'd made love too much at the Irish cottage. He kissed and soothed Stella between the bouts of recurring pain, and helped to wipe her face with cool cloths soaked in eau-de-Cologne.

'Bear down.' It was the only thing left to say, and she wasn't doing it. She was ramrod-stiff, resisting everything. There was an operation, he knew, but it meant cutting the mother's body open, and Stella would be left with a scar. He wouldn't endure the thought of it. There were forceps, weren't there? They must send for the doctor and he could use those.

The doctor came, examined Stella and asked how long ago the labour had begun. He gave her something to sedate her, then dismissed everybody from the room but Hannah. 'You will be all right now, my darling,' Gareth murmured, kissing her. 'They are going to take it away.'

'Yes. Please, take it away.' She must be drowsy. He left her with the doctor and Hannah, and waited miserably in the next room. How could he live without Stella? He'd been neglectful, and at the same time too eager. This must never happen again. In future, he would love her like a flower, a precious relic; he wouldn't ever enter her again. He walked up and down in anguish till word came; the child was born, a little girl.

They had twisted her out blue-faced at last with the forceps' grip hard on her skull. This was covered already with little curls like snail-shells, and would dry out to a fair gold. 'She'll be the image of her mother,' said Hannah aloud, and Stella, half-conscious, seemed to breathe more easily. They saw to her and the child, and laid it at last in the pearwood cradle no longer inhabited by Brian Laracor. A wet-nurse was sent for, as her ladyship had said she didn't want to lose her figure. The woman had to be discreet, as such women guess when a birth is not premature at all. However the comings and goings of Sir Gareth were not known in detail to all and sundry. He waited till he knew his wife was safe, then took himself off again.

Next day, the baby was seen to have a severe

bruise on her temple where the forceps had dragged her out. When her eyes opened they were likewise seen, after the first few days when all babies' eyes are blue, to be an unchildlike grey-green. It must be from some forebear; neither of her parents had eyes that colour.

\*     \*     \*

Stella was never fond of her daughter, but she was unmaternal likewise to young Brian Laracor. Both children grew, but whereas the boy continued as he ought, the little girl, called Sabrina, was found to be deaf. This meant that she would never learn to speak.

# Part Two

# CHAPTER ONE

Stella was sitting in the folly at the further side of the artificial lake at Leys, staring beyond Sabrina's small subdued figure to where swans glided and peacocks strutted. Just now there had been, miracle of miracles, a spread tail; all the colours of the rainbow in a great shining fan. If only Gareth had been here to see it with her! Its owner had closed it abruptly after moments in the way they did, and had gone trailing off. As for the peahen, it reminded her of Mrs Comstock, and the forthcoming meeting today. They'd asked Stella lately to rejoin it, and she could think of no reason to refuse.

She knew she hadn't wanted to refuse. She knew a great many things about herself she hadn't known before.

*     *     *

Pilar, upstairs, was busy polishing the glass window-panes at a place where she could see the summer-house and its occupants. Presently she happened to come to the pane which was bottle-glass. It twisted and distorted the view, including that of the two figures beyond the lake. Briefly, they became no longer a golden-haired woman and her child, but grotesques. It was almost as though the ill-concealed dislike Stella felt for little Sabrina had taken shape, altering appearances to another kind of reality.

Pilar drew sharply away from the pane. It told too much truth. Once the glass was plain again the evil vanished, or was the real evil an everyday sight? Miss Stella punished the child frequently without cause, as though it relieved her in some way. Only this morning Sabrina's harsh dreary crying had sounded again from upstairs: her mother was whipping her. It happened too often, and a servant couldn't interfere, or even ask why. By now, the little creature was again passive and silent, her tears dried for the time. Any chance visitor would perceive only beautiful Lady Seaborne and her little daughter, the latter suitably dressed and correctly holding her doll. Nobody would notice that the child didn't care to sit down.

What had happened to Miss Stella? There had been a time when she would not have whipped her dog. She'd never struck Talley in all the days in Dublin. She'd been as sweet as honey then.

She herself, Pilar the good servant, must forget, not ask herself questions, get on with her polishing. Of what use to allow a twisted view through bottle-glass to remain in her mind?

Yet it stayed. Often at nights, after that, Pilar would think of it despite herself, lying alone in her bed, recalling that instant's revealed and ugly truth, seen through a distorting window.

*  *  *

She saw Stella meantime put up a hand to tidy a straggle of her hair. There had been a light breeze ruffling the lake, disturbing her ladyship's coiffure. Otherwise it was a fine day, and the county might call. Her ladyship wouldn't want to look blowsy, after this morning's exertions.

As for Stella, her mouth was set; as a rule it had grown looser lately. She was thinking of how Sabrina's doll had been a present to the child from Gareth last time he'd been home. He'd bought it on impulse in a shop in Grafton Street, near where an old woman still played her harp for coins. It had fair hair, the doll, he said, like Sabrina's. He thought far too much about Sabrina, not enough about herself. The doll must have been expensive. It had two dresses, a petticoat and matching lace-trimmed drawers. On Gareth's giving it to Sabrina the little devil had pulled up the dress and petticoat, pulled down the drawers and begun to smack the doll. It was her way of telling tales, as she couldn't speak.

Gareth had been horrified. 'You don't whip her, Stella?' He was fond of his supposed daughter, and not being often at home thought her perfect, no doubt. Stella had explained that when Sabrina attempted to speak, the noise was so harsh it couldn't be lived with. The only thing had been to smack her out of it. 'In any case, she's wilful. You spoil her, and she expects it from everyone.'

By now—she had been whipped again afterwards for that when he'd gone away— Sabrina had learned the value of silence. She stood passively holding the doll, both of them in matching summer dresses. Her fair curls had been gathered in a knot on top of her head with ribbon. She was no doubt a very pretty little girl, for what good it might do. Gareth had bought her a paint-box, and had shown her how to paint little houses, with doors and windows and chimneys with smoke coming out. He had tried to teach her to read from flannel books, with the cat sitting on the mat and suchlike. He had held her small hand and taught her how to spell her name, *Sabrina fair.* Did he trouble to remember the long-ago waltz? He'd been home again once for almost two months when the Dublin editor briefly found an assistant: and hadn't ever lain with her. 'No, my darling, we must guard your health,' he would say. It was Sabrina's fault for having been born, with such agony he couldn't risk more.

Stella looked at her daughter with sidelong hatred. Oddly, one forgot the pains of birth, terrible as they had no doubt been. To have a husband one loved who wouldn't be more than a brother was much harder to bear.

Stella moved restlessly. She yawned, then her mouth resumed its customary discontented droop. She was putting on weight these days; she took no exercise. Her breasts were the size of melons; she let her hands lift them absently. She looked by now, and knew it, Juno rather than Aphrodite. She had been used once in bed in a way she couldn't forget.

Her clothes had ceased to fit. She had had new ones made, and slapped the dressmaker when the pins pricked. It hadn't been the woman's fault: what was the matter with her, Stella Seaborne? As for her mind, it was empty even of accomplishments. She'd never liked reading, although Papa had used to try to get her to take an interest in the paper. As for embroidery, she couldn't be troubled with it. She liked it well enough when the county called. They were no longer as condescending, and it passed the time.

Otherwise, she played cards with Pilar or else whipped Sabrina. Those were two ways of seeing the days go by, but the nights were different, full of ennui and worse. To face it, Stella had to admit to herself that bodily desire troubled her increasingly. If Gareth had been a husband to her again it might have been different, but then again it might not. He'd always been too gentle with her; she knew it now. She wanted a man who would master her, fill her. She wanted the sheriff back in her bed.

It was shameful, and when she was alone she would handle her own breasts to try to relieve it, the increasing longing. That was worse; she would think then of how his thick hands had pounded and kneaded them, his grim lips mouthing them, his vast parts thrusting in her again and again till she wanted to cry out. He had stretched and achieved her repeatedly against her will; what might not happen now, when she was willing?

She was glad, at any rate, they had asked her to rejoin the charity-committee. When he was near, if he came close, her knees would weaken and turn to water. She was a shameful woman, no doubt. Where had she got it? Papa had never been like that, had never gone after women; and she couldn't remember her mother. Nobody had spoken about her, except to say, on asking, that she was dead. What had she been like? Had Papa, in bed, satisfied her? Had her own conception been as it should?

One could never ask such things. The only relief was to whip the child Stern had given her, whip it on its bare bottom till it howled. That was unkind, no doubt. It was as well Gareth wasn't often here to ask questions. He had a kind heart. It wasn't that she didn't love him. If only—.

She was still a desirable woman, after all. Soon, after luncheon, the carriage would come, and take her, with Pilar, to town: to the charity meeting. There was that to look forward to. Nobody had called. Again, Stella tidied her hair.

## CHAPTER TWO

At that particular meeting, Mrs Comstock, who naturally had never resigned, sat beside her ladyship and noted Stella's ill-concealed restlessness. It didn't seem as if her ladyship took in a word of what the sheriff was talking about, whether it was the correction-house accounts or the state of the almshouses or, what no doubt interested him particularly, the discovery of woodworm in the pews of the sectarian chapel; funds would have to be raised to eradicate that. Abigail Comstock let her mind wander back to the sayings of her late husband, who had been a schoolmaster and a native of Suffolk. He had been given to sudden revelations of esoteric knowledge and she remembered his saying that there was a special variety of woodworm that only lived in Suffolk and made oval holes instead of round ones, and why the Almighty should have disposed this phenomenon as he had, it was difficult to say.

There wouldn't be any point in telling the meeting that, as this wasn't Suffolk. Abigail let her gaze rest on the verbose colossus presiding in its dark clothes, exuding masculinity in a way that was hardly proper. It was impossible not to think of the parish bull.

\*       \*       \*

Stern himself was holding forth about woodworm, but almost openly surveying Stella. The feasibility of once more enjoying her luscious body, perhaps more than once, obsessed him afresh now she sat there, outwardly conforming but inwardly, as he was aware, fully sensible of his near presence. This might well be; she would never have spent another such night in her life. The sheriff's renewed urgings were mixed, by now, with condescension; all women were the same, and in the time taken for nature to repair Stella's body after the child's birth, natural desire would have been renewed also. He was aware, from the earlier experience, that there were things he had taught young Lady Seaborne that marriage hadn't, and probably in the circumstances never would. It would be beneficial to her in all ways to repeat the lesson. He had the strong notion, seeing her disquiet, that she would not, by now, refuse.

With civic courtesy, at the end of the meeting, he addressed her ladyship and asked if she would care to inspect the minutes a little more closely? They were in his office.

Abigail watched as Stella, her face expressionless, went in. There might be nothing more to it, after all. The door closed behind them, however, and she heard the key turn in the lock.

*       *       *

Sabrina had begun to wet her drawers if Mama was anywhere near, and at times when she wasn't. Even Pilar was cross, and wagged her finger. It made everything worse with Mama for the time, and she told the servants not to waste clean linen. 'She can do without 'em till she learns to behave herself.'

Sabrina, left naked beneath her petticoats, began to hide in one place Mama wouldn't find her; Sir Eldred's old gilded coach, kept in the back of the stables. She would go there sometimes even when she hadn't been whipped. She liked to pretend that she was driving imaginary horses, like the real ones Stevens used when he drove Papa and Mama in their carriage. She would pretend to be holding reins, and that the red velvet seats were new and didn't smell of mould, and the coach itself kept bright and shining. When she'd been punished, of course, she would go and cry in it. It was in this state that Stevens came upon her one day in the course of cleaning out the loose-boxes. Miss Sabrina's eyes and her little nose were red, her face wet with tears, and everyone knew what often happened to her; her ladyship was too strict when Sir Gareth wasn't at home.

She was lying across the seat face down, but had turned to look at him, and the sight moved Stevens to a certain pity, not without the prospect of some reward. He slid into the coach and pulled up the child's skirts, revealing her sore little scarlet bottom; he hadn't expected to find it bare. He began to stroke and soothe it, and soon Miss Sabrina stopped sobbing, and didn't seem to mind his strokings. It wasn't possible to speak to her so that she would understand, but Stevens managed without words: from the first such visit to others, by degrees going further with her, not yet as far as he hoped to go; it was like breaking in a little filly, which he knew very well how to do. By that time, her ladyship seemed to whip Miss Sabrina less often; she would be driven up to town instead a great deal in the carriage, returning flushed and vague. Stevens would pass the waiting time thinking profitably about Miss Sabrina. He hadn't, himself, had much luck with the girls; they laughed at him and called him rat-face. He knew, accordingly, what to do with Miss Sabrina, not causing her to look at him much.

It rested there meantime. That Pilar had sharp eyes, and he mustn't risk his job.

Sabrina, after he had shown her something, wondered what Papa's was like. Papa liked to kiss and fondle her as well. Men were different, evidently. Meantime she'd stopped

106

wetting herself, but Mama didn't notice, being out by then a great deal, and she didn't order drawers to be put back on Sabrina, who was happy without them; they got in the way, and by then she liked Stevens to kiss and fondle and stroke and pry.

*    *    *

Pilar was sitting as usual on the reception bench while the customary meeting went on at the town hall. Mrs Comstock and Mrs Yeoman attended, also as usual, and her ladyship. The meetings were held by now once or twice weekly, and not all of them could invariably attend. Her ladyship was in fact the most faithful member, with a number of officials including, without fail, the sheriff. At times, Pilar herself wasn't sure who was present and who wasn't; there were several entries, one at the side and another at the back, where Stevens used to take round the carriage to be out of the way of street traffic. Often there was a long wait, sometimes more than an hour; whatever had they all found to talk about? Her ladyship naturally didn't discuss what had taken place.

In its way, that was understandable. On emergence from a meeting some time ago now, Pilar had noticed that Miss Stella's bodice wasn't correctly fastened, as it had certainly been when they set out. One of the fastenings had been replaced too low, the other too high. It was the only sign of what might, after all, have happened. The sheriff didn't come out to the hall. He might have been absent altogether, except for the matter of her ladyship's bodice. Pilar kept silent; as silent as little Sabrina, except when she still howled.

\*　　\*　　\*

Mrs Comstock could have said more. After the meetings she would take tea by custom with the sheriff's sister, and they talked about this and that; her ladyship didn't join them, but went in to discuss further business again, about the minutes, with the sheriff. Once this would have caused envy in the breast of Mrs Comstock; now, she was merely curious. On one occasion Mrs Yeoman was called away briefly on some matter, and Abigail darted towards the door through which Lady Seabome and Sheriff Hezekiah had by custom vanished. Examination of the minutes always seemed to go on after everyone had left; she'd seen Stevens still sitting at the carriage, staring at the reins, while Pilar sat patiently on in the outer hall. The inner room was beyond the meeting-place, and as the best way of ascertaining what went on there Mrs Comstock put her eye to the keyhole, having listened first to make sure nobody was coming abruptly out. There was silence in the room, and an opened door led into a room further beyond still, whose purpose could till now only be guessed at. Meantime, on a chair, lay her ladyship's gown, stays and chemise; her high-heeled shoes were neatly placed below. More need not either be said or guessed at. Mrs Comstock hugged her secret to her bosom in private titillation. She might have known there was more to it than minutes.

## CHAPTER THREE

The dowager, Sir Eldred's widow, was found one afternoon by Hannah with her fingers stilled above a grimy snowdrift of torn newspapers. Otherwise she looked much the same as usual. Hannah went downstairs to tell them her mistress was dead.

'Poor soul, she would know nothing different,' she said, and tears rose in her eyes less for her late charge than for herself. 'You'll not turn me out, my lady?' she begged Stella. 'I've served with her since they sent me from the correction-house, and would hardly know how to begin with any other place.'

Stella assured her that they would keep her on, if only to be company for Pilar. Hannah had always thought Pilar sly, knowing what she must: but it was a relief not to have to go somewhere strange.

The dowager's funeral took place, presided over by a bishop. There was a great attendance of the county, who came to honour the corpse they had not troubled to visit while alive. It was known that her old ladyship had become reclusive since she grew blind. Heads were shaken by those who recalled Sir Eldred and his unbridled ways, pertaining more to the old century than the new. The squire was unavoidably absent, and sent his excuses.

Women did not, as was customary, attend the interment, which took place beside the late dowager's husband's remains in the ugly memorial vault up the hill. Converging instead at Leys House for madeira and cake, they were later joined by the bishop. He sat benignly with Sabrina on his knee, as he liked children. She stared at his purple vest and began to play with his crucifix. Stella raised a finger.

'Do not prevent her,' said the bishop, who thought the child a little angel; a pity she was unable to hear or speak. 'Our Lord said "Suffer the little children" and would not have minded his image being touched.' He then began to talk about Australia, where he had spent many years before promotion to a diocese. The reason was that the sheriff's sister, Mrs Yeoman, sat with her crony Mrs Comstock close by. The sheriff himself, having attended the funeral, had no need now to visit Leys.

'Your name is one frequently met with out there,' remarked the bishop, sipping his madeira and feeding Sabrina small pieces of cake. 'In fact your son Henry, whom I knew in Parramatta, mentioned that his mother lived at Leys in England. It is a small world, is it not? He resembles your brother the sheriff very closely. When I saw him he was growing into a fine boy, with a disposition which suits the life out there very well.' He then began to speak of the terrible conditions endured by convicts, who were often sent out for very little and remained, with one renewed sentence after another, for the rest of their lives. 'By then, of course, they have often accustomed themselves to the conditions, and once they are freed find employment and even buy land. Nevertheless I knew a young woman who was sent to Botany Bay for stealing a piece of cloth, and once there her morals sadly became lowered. The forms of punishment under the present law can be excessive and ill-judged.'

He finished his cake, oblivious of the confusion of the sheriff's sister, who had crimsoned like a peony and had found herself unable to partake of her madeira. Abigail Comstock, with one more secret to hug to her bosom, wore the expression of a cat who had swallowed cream. So there was a Yeoman son! It had never been mentioned. Afterwards she remarked to Henry's mother that perhaps one day he would make a visit home.

After the guests had gone Sabrina was returned to the terrace, where she and Brian Laracor had been told to remain quietly. He was in a black suit with a white starched collar, in honour of the occasion. She, of course, didn't know why so many people had been there. However the old gentleman in the purple vest had been kind. Shortly, after they had all departed, Brian went to his tutor and Sabrina took herself to the place where she liked to hide, Sir Eldred's old coach in the stables. It was still lined with crimson velvet going rotten, but the outside was gold. She liked to sit in front and pretend she was holding the reins of long-dead horses, making them trot.

\*　　　\*　　　\*

Stella stood watching the departing carriages. Renewed solitude brought on her ever-increasing craving for Stern. This was Tuesday, and in the ordinary way there would have been a town hall meeting. The thought of what, till now, had always happened afterwards brought the familiar weakness to Stella's knees, a spreading of desire through her whole body that simply wasn't excusable. She was being changed and consumed, and knew it, but couldn't stop. He'd said last time that the situation might affect his position if it was discovered, and that it would be more discreet if they met, not, as till now, in the town hall inner office, but up at the correction-house; there was a further room which was private. It happened to be the one where he interviewed arriving orphans, and Stella had resented the lumping together with them even more than the statement that his position would be affected if her visits to him were known. What about her own position? 'It's on your back,' he had replied crudely. She was afraid of him, a bitch afraid of its master; in a way still loathed him, yet needed him increasingly. The correction-house was, as he had said, private. Mrs Yeoman would certainly suspect and assist. They must go on pretending elsewhere that it was a consultation about orphans. She, Stella Seaborne, was beginning to be accustomed to deceit, to anything. If Gareth had only stayed at home!

\*     \*     \*

Pilar was playing chess with Sir Gareth. She made the moves in a dream, having just learned them from him. Once a week she'd polish the unfolded board, with its chequer pattern of onyx and ivory set into a little table. It had belonged to Sir Eldred, and was old, like most of the things there. The chessmen, ivory and red, were kept in a box. He'd shown her, Sir Gareth, earlier, having assembled them on the board: queens and kings, knights red and white, bishops, castles: and the different ways they all moved. It was something she'd never expected to know about. Miss Stella was out, had been still so by evening, and before dinner he'd been starting to play by himself. He was only home for two days; you'd think her ladyship could have spared the time to stay with him.

She, Pilar, had been passing beyond the room, and he'd called out to her to ask if she knew how to play. He'd have called out to anyone. He was looking at the chessmen still, no doubt thinking of Miss Stella. She herself had answered as expected.

'No, sir, but I dare say I can learn.'

She was quick at learning such things; that and cards. Cards, however, were not as slow. This game gave time to think. She watched Gareth's head bent over the board, seeing and loving every fine line that was beginning to show in his face; small lines of worry beneath the eyes, a thought of future deep ones between nose and mouth. It was a fine face, and would have suited a coin; she knew those well enough, and the kings' profiles, all four Georges in their different wigs and crowns, and after that old Billy.

Crowns. There was a young queen now.

She herself was no longer quite so young. She was still wearing her apron. Her hands, when they touched the chessmen, were rough with work, not like Miss Stella's white ones.

114

All the same, he seemed at ease with her, for a change: no doubt he'd forgotten who she was, being intent on the moves. They'd played a simple return, and he went on to show her some of the subtler combinations. Then the carriage arrived outside, heard in the autumn dusk. Gareth looked up in hope: Stella had come home!

She entered the room, beautiful and triumphant, still in her cloak. She flung it off, came straight across and kissed him. He forgot the game of chess. 'Pilar, you may go,' said Stella pleasantly. 'I can finish the game.'

Pilar rose and went out of the room. Once in the passage again, she clenched her fists against her apron. Anger rising in her she didn't know she could feel. *Pilar, you may go.* The pride of hidalgos, of her half-known blood, rose uncontrolled for instants; supposing she went to the kitchen, got a long sharp knife, came back and plunged it between her ladyship's much-handled breasts and watched the crimson life spurt out of her? She'd come in like a great queen cat, sidling home after its time with the tom. Her blue eyes had been slumbrous, sated between languid lids. The meeting must have finished its business four or five hours ago. There was hardly a pretence, any longer, that they were anything but an excuse for Stella's whoredoms. She was a bad bitch, like her mother. Sir Gareth wouldn't see it.

He would break his heart, after all, if Miss Stella came to harm. She herself must forget about the knife. She was a servant, and had learned to play chess. That meant you had to learn patience. How she'd loved the close sight of him, this evening, with the curtains drawn and lamps lit early! They'd shown her a few silver-grey hairs among the cinnamon. He hadn't noticed her, or that her eyes had feasted on him.

Later she heard them go in to dinner, then later still bid one another goodnight. They slept in separate rooms. Pilar tried to remember the moves in chess. It would have needed more time, however: much more time.

\*      \*      \*

Stella had in fact left the correction-house at a quarter to four: there hadn't been any meeting. Stern, in the back room, had used her hard since two. She had been too greatly afraid, as usual, to ask him to be careful. He wouldn't listen, and she knew he preached, in his chapel sermons—she hadn't been, there were things one couldn't be known to do—that God had told Eve she must labour and bear, as a punishment for sin, and that that was what women were for. She was very much afraid, again, that it might have happened. If he wouldn't stop, there was one thing to be done. She'd thought of it once or twice, and this time had seen about it, with results that could not have been expected, but which by now didn't matter. She no longer recognised herself.

In the town's high street was a black jutting sign whose worn gilt letters proclaimed J. Payne and Sons, Apothecaries. Below hung a gilt mortar and pestle. One didn't, these days, call them anything but chemists, but there they had been for three generations. The present owner, Mr Joseph Payne, was said to be a likely choice for next sheriff. However he in no way resembled the existing holder of the office if one judged from outward appearances. Narrowness and propriety were written in his every aspect, as befitted a glorified shopkeeper.

Had Stella known, Joe Payne was consumed with envy of the sheriff, and considered himself in every way a worthier occupant of the civic dignity. Stern's habits were becoming widely whispered about, and Nemesis would overtake him in the end. Payne himself was a neat small thin man, with a straggling goatee long turned grey. His appearance was rendered less nebulous by rimless spectacles, which had the effect of concealing his thoughts from the world. His hands were small, dry, precise, and trained to measure prescriptions. He employed one assistant, an intelligent orphan from the correction-house. His parsimony was suited by this arrangement.

For the aforementioned possibility, Stella

had had herself driven up one day to see him. It was becoming advisable to consult somebody, though she might, this time, again be mistaken. She instructed Stevens to draw up a few doors along, opposite the boot and shoe shop. It wasn't that, like the celebrated Mrs Gilpin, she was worried lest all should think her proud. It was simply that she didn't want to be seen to go into the chemist's. It wouldn't have been advisable to ask the servants, even Pilar, to obtain this particular prescription. As it was, she didn't know exactly what to ask for. Mr Payne would no doubt give advice.

She found herself in the shop, with its myriad tiny drawers set against the wall, each one bearing its mysterious gilded abbreviation about whatever was inside. In the window had been two old-fashioned glass alembics, one filled with red, the other with blue, liquid. Sadie, the former orphan who helped Mr Payne and kept house—he was a bachelor— rose up from behind the counter, placing her thin hands squarely on its mahogany surface, and asked what she might do for her ladyship.

'I had rather hoped to see Mr Payne,' said Stella. However that personage, on hearing her name uttered, had already emerged from his inner sanctum, where he kept his accounts and receipts, also a number of unused alembics from old days, and a horsehair sofa.

'My lady, permit me.' He ushered Stella into

the sanctum, closing the door. That was, at least, satisfactory; she didn't want that girl overhearing everything.

On hearing her stammered request the chemist shook his grey head gently, glasses gleaming. 'We are not allowed to, my lady.'

'I had a bad time at my daughter's birth. I don't want more children.'

'Well—'

Behind that word lay a morass of feeling. Like his rival the sheriff, Mr Payne had gazed from afar on the beauty of her ladyship, and like David with Bathsheba, desired her. As a rule, and always with prudence, he could persuade Sadie to oblige, but that was a humdrum business adequately made safe by the very prescription Lady Seaborne was enquiring about now: its chief ingredient was extract of pennyroyal. He always made a point of dosing Sadie, generally on Thursdays. The thought of likewise dosing her ladyship almost induced a state of delirium, but Payne kept his head. A bargain might perhaps be politely struck. He was well aware, as several now were despite everything, of the real state of affairs between her ladyship and Hezekiah Stern.

Stern could not presume to own the world's womanhood outright. Mr Payne proceeded to make the situation clear. As Stella listened in incredulity, she felt the dry fingers travel up her forearm, then clasp themselves about her breast. It still tingled from Stern's recent handlings.

'Perhaps a little encounter,' vouchsafed Mr Payne. He added that he would not take money. As if in a dream, she heard, first, his instructions to Sadie to deal with customers and take any messages and prescriptions meantime. Then, as before, the key turned in the lock. Stella felt the goatee tickle her neck.

Presently Sadie herself, unoccupied, took her ear away from the keyhole. The alembics had commenced to rattle long ago. The old goat and her ladyship were at it on the horsehair sofa. She herself remembered, with wistful longing, her initiation with Sheriff Stern. There was a man, if you liked. If she'd been handsome like her ladyship, it might have happened again, but it hadn't; and she'd been apprenticed instead to Payne, who didn't have anything of the kind worth mentioning. Lady Seaborne was welcome to it.

\*     \*     \*

By the time of Pilar's chess game, Mr Payne had been in the habit, for some time, of dosing her ladyship of necessity once a month. His own transports had ceased to be prudent. Outwardly, they could have been certified as his: tck, tck; this is delightful—quite refreshing dear me, tck—you really have glorious, er— tck—I assure you, this is an occasion to which I always look forward—tck. Tck. There.

120

He might, she used to think, as well have been a spinster. The encounters didn't matter. The doses he gave her afterwards were black, tasted bitter, and worked. Stern could excel himself now, without its worrying her afterwards. It seemed to irritate him, and spur him on, that she'd stayed as she was.

Had she known, Stern had again meantime selected a skinny and unwilling orphan, who obliged him by falling pregnant immediately. He had been troubled lest his fecundity was becoming affected; now, it appeared to be Stella's fault. There must be something wrong with her: and she was beginning to be insatiable.

This last was Sadie's doing. On one occasion Mr Payne had requested her, as he was greatly occupied, to prepare the usual dose for her ladyship. Sadie smiled quietly, and left out the pennyroyal. Instead—the mixture was black anyway—she put in a good pinch of Spanish fly. Whatever it was her ladyship wanted, she'd want it all the time after *that*.

Mr Payne himself continued to be increasingly well suited. On more than one occasion now, he had become unusually flustered. Her ladyship was so desirable he had forgotten himself. Tck, tck. It was a mercy there was the dosage, with the squire so seldom at home.

Gareth, back again in Dublin, was having a dream. Black and ivory squares rose before him, and across them, waltzing, came a red knight. The equine head and neck nodded, twisted, moved straight and then sideways. Somewhere there was music, but it was not a part of the dream. A woman's hands came out, one grasping the red knight, the other his own. That should not happen. He had blocked out Pilar from his mind, had made himself forget what she meant. She was a servant, nothing more now, with worn hands that did daily work: yet they had made the moves sensibly. He was glad she was there to look after Stella and Sabrina.

He thought of Stella with unbearable longing. She wouldn't come into the dream, with the music; they were separate now, part of another life. He must remember it, and how perfect it had been; and there was still Sabrina. She must be protected from all harm, unable as she was to hear or speak; but she could understand, pretty little creature, the image of Stella.

Gareth woke in the dawn, and put on his dressing-gown. It would pass the time to write an article for the paper.

*　　*　　*

Pilar could hear Stella walking up and down, up and down. It was late at night, and she couldn't have slept. In the end, hearing her moan, Pilar went in to her. She found Stella holding her own full breasts, weighing them, walking and moaning. When Pilar came she merely turned her head, and didn't stop.

'What is it?' Pilar asked. They had been friends once, rather than mistress and servant. There might be some of it left. Stella continued to hold and weigh her breasts. 'I can't help myself,' she said. 'You know what goes on. I want it now all the time.'

It was her first admission that Pilar might know anything. 'Why not go to Dublin?' Pilar said. 'Once before, that consoled you.' She couldn't bear to think of it, but it might be the answer.

'It wouldn't now. He won't sleep with me since that child's birth. That's partly why I hate the child. In any case I don't want Gareth now in such a way. I want Stern. I want him here, in my bed.'

'You can't have that,' said Pilar firmly. 'I won't let him in.'

'You let him in once. I thought I loathed it. Now I need it. I need it all the time, I tell you. You don't have feelings, Pilar. You take things as they come.'

Don't I? Pilar thought. In the end she got Miss Stella to bed with hot milk and a sedative. Perhaps it would make her sleep.

However she would be the same tomorrow. What would happen next, nobody knew.

## CHAPTER FOUR

The high sheriff had, as already explained, found it more convenient to let his stately trousers fall in the private office of the correction-house than in the town hall. Other business might intervene there, and he had begun to grow wary of his civic reputation, so frequently did the fall of his trousers these days take place.

The indefinable smell of institutions on behalf of poverty did not trouble him any more than, in such ways, it ever had. The orphans, including the bulging one he had some time since encountered, were safely sewing calico beyond two doors. His sister kept guard beyond one. As by arrangement—she was known to take a singular interest in the welfare of the orphans and to visit them once or twice a week for a long time now—the squire's lady lay, naked, on an elderly chaise-longue. It had at sundry times borne the weight of the sheriff and some assailed orphan or other, and it bore his weight again now. In course of ensuing recreation it knocked, as always, against the wall, and the knocking reminded a listening Mrs Yeoman of the time she'd spent on board ship to Australia. Now that the secret of Henry's existence had been made public knowledge by the bishop, her fear of her brother had lessened. Hezekiah was only a man after all; listen to them both at it now. She'd given up being surprised by her ladyship. You could tell from her bitten lips, when she came out again dressed in haste afterwards, that she'd controlled herself lest she be heard by third parties, namely oneself. The orphans were too far away, though nothing would have surprised them either. The harvest of babies for apprenticeship had, for some time now, thinned, the sheriff being kept fully occupied in higher social spheres.

The sheriff as usual was taking his pleasure without stint, only half aware of the submissive writhings of the body of Juno beneath him. In mythology, that goddess had been possessed by few except Jove. He was aware that he was fortunate, also that he was doing a favour to a young woman which need not be underestimated and, by now, was not. The sheriff continued to heed the Bible's instructions not to waste his seed; for whatever reason, she hadn't conceived again since the girl's birth, but it was in any case of no importance how many more children Stella Seaborne might or might not bear him; by law they were her husband's. The sheriff could therefore continue to disclaim responsibility and pass the hour in scripturally approved abandonment.

There was no doubt, he thought, savouring it, that the frequent handling of her flesh had matured and increased it; by now, she was a plumply desirable young matron. He brought her through the familiar stages to the peak of wanting to cry out at last, yet not daring to. It showed a proper awareness of their relative positions. It had been evident, from the day of the resuscitated charity meetings, that Stella required his services in a way which might have been expected; the husband was seldom at home. She could after all have called out for help in the inner room at the town hall where the minutes were kept that time he'd invited her in afterwards to inspect them. She had hesitated on the threshold, then crossed it; and had remained silent when she watched his hand turn the key in the lock.

After that renewed and satisfactory episode, the others had become customary, in fact increasingly frequent. The husband should be at home oftener for his own good. Stella's subservience at all times beneath him, nowadays, proved his accustomed self-esteem to be thoroughly merited. As a stallion he had no rival.

The hour passed profitably. At the end, when she turned her back to dress, having put on her chemise first, she bent to pull up her filmy stockings, secured as they were at the tops by delicate pale-blue silk garters embroidered with miniature rosebuds. The act of bending caused the chemise to reveal more than was intended. Stern reached out his spatulate finger and thumb, causing them to meet in the delectable flesh of Stella's backside. He then went on to fresh discovery. The squire's lady knew by now, after all, who was master.

Beyond the crack of the rear door, Stevens the coachman watched avidly as he always did. He was able to imitate the sheriff only in so far as passing his tongue across his lips.

## CHAPTER FIVE

Stevens had already begun to console himself with the child Sabrina. He hadn't gone as far yet as he hoped to go; she was still too young, but could be trained in the way she must perform, like a little bloodstock foal got ready early. Her deafness meant she couldn't tell anyone like that Pilar what was happening; the thing was to get her used to it, gradually, till he could do as he wanted with her. She had, after all, the promise of a hot little tail; her mother's antics through the crack of the door were one thing, and the sheriff was almost certainly her father. He himself was of the stock of old Sir Eldred, and hadn't been left what he ought. He could take payment this way. His mother would protect him if there was a complaint of any kind. She'd say he was with her at the time anything was said to have happened.

Meanwhile he had got into the habit of easing himself into the old gilded coach with the velvet lining, where little Miss Sabrina hid from her mother and all the rest. He, Stevens, had stroked her sore little bottom often enough, pretending to make it better, and had kissed her. He would caress her bare arms, sliding his hands up to feel the smooth place above her elbows, inside her bodice, then under her gown to do the same to her legs, and the bare place above her stockings, then the place between. She had grown used to him. One day he had shown her something more, and made her stroke it. She thought it was a game, and after that they always did it. She often came to the stables to hide in the coach. Even Pilar didn't see any harm in it, having other things to do. Soon, he'd do more to little Miss Sabrina, but not yet. He was a man who believed in patience, in waiting till she was older, though not much. The thought consoled him while he continued to watch her ladyship cavorting with the sheriff; one day, he and Sabrina would do the same. She didn't, after all, know anyone else to speak of, and never would. He'd got in first. He was pleased with himself. There was plenty of time.

*　　　*　　　*

Pilar had tried, as far as it might be done, to take a mother's place with the child Sabrina, as her own mother continued actively to dislike her. Pilar continued likewise aware of the relationship between Stella and the sheriff, Sabrina's real father, and that it had by no means run its course. She had made herself cease to think of it. So much was not what it seemed: her own lack of her son should have been solaced by Sabrina's dependence on her, and was not. She confessed to herself that she didn't altogether take to Sabrina: even so young, there was something there that shouldn't be. That time she'd bared the doll Sir Gareth brought her, and smacked it, had been calculating, not like a child. Children took what came, even injustice, and put up with it. Perhaps Sabrina, in her closed world of silence, was no longer childlike: or perhaps she resembled the sheriff, her father. At that rate there would be trouble later on.

Pilar tried to remember her own childhood, now very far away, less in time than because of all that had happened since. Her father had been kind, the *madre* not always so: she could have a vicious temper. Oneself was, therefore, a mixture of one and the other, and the Spanish part must be controlled: she did her best. All the same—and she smiled to herself—one thing common to both Spaniards and Irish was the ability to love, fiercely, proudly, and despite all odds. Pilar hugged that certainty to herself in a silence almost like Sabrina's. She hadn't ever given away, by word or look, her abiding love for Sir Gareth.

And Stella? She was becoming like her mother Maeve, who'd run off with O'Halloran, leaving her husband and baby. No doubt Maeve, descended from lustful vikings, had had golden hair.

## CHAPTER SIX

Some days later the high sheriff sat, agreeably sated, writing notes at his desk in the town hall. The memory of Stella's varied enticements occupied half his mind if they no longer filled his hands. They no longer, if they ever had, interrupted the course of official duty, however, and the written report was evenly and efficiently rendered. In fact Stella's physical possession was so much a part of his mentality that by now Stern took it for granted. She was certainly the finest piece of flesh he had ever handled, but all flesh is grass. Of late it had become evident that she relied on him, and this irritated Hezekiah's private aspect like a recurrent fly. He himself would be possessed by nobody, in particular no woman. He was not yet prepared to dismiss Stella from his life, but she must by no means become an inconvenience in it. If a fly landed again and again despite brushing off, it must be persuaded into a vulnerable position and then crushed. This was, for the moment, a cloud no bigger than a man's hand. Meantime there was other business.

A clerk, however, appeared at the door and said Lady Seaborne was waiting, and would like a word with the sheriff. Stern frowned a little. Stella was not in the habit of coming here now, and he had a meeting of council shortly. He told the man to show her ladyship into the smaller reception room, finished his notes, then after a further deliberate pause went in to see her. She flung herself at him, putting back her veil.

'Oh God, I think I'm going to have a child again, and it's yours.' That prim old maid of a chemist, with his futile thrustings! The dosage hadn't worked this time. She'd tried everything.

Stern was coldly angry. Her voice might have been heard beyond the door. Did she think she was so much better than most? The Lord saw fit for a woman to conceive or not. He had no desire to play King David and kill Uriah. *Am I to go home in comfort, and lie with my wife, when there is a battle to be won?* Stern found to his irritation that he could not recall the exact words as they occurred in Holy Writ. He took Stella by the shoulders.

'It is inconvenient for you to come here; do

not do so again. Send for your husband, and induce him to do his duty.' Sir Gareth hadn't been home now for some time; the matter could become awkward. He himself had almost used the new word co-operation, which she wouldn't understand; it had recently been brought into being by the Society of Equitable Pioneers. Stern liked to keep up with such information.

He became aware that Stella was drumming at him with her fists and that tears were pouring down her face. 'How dare you mention him?' she was screaming. 'How dare you?'

The matter was becoming an embarrassment. He decided to get rid of her; after all he had had his fill of her by now. The husband must be persuaded to return. 'Whoredoms,' he said, 'are by statute punished in this town in the way you already know of. Nobody was more aware of the fact than the late Sir Eldred Seaborne. You must acquire a father for your child by the usual means. In your own and your husband's position, that would appear to be advisable.'

He dealt with her drumming fists by taking them in one hand and propelling her towards the door. She had begun to scream and sob uncontrollably.

'He won't do it to me—he won't do it since the birth.'

She must be silenced. He slapped her face,

then put a hand inside his stout belt, easing it. 'By God, if you disturb me again in my office I'll leather your bare bum till you have to kneel in your carriage going home. Get out.'

Fluency of language came to him from on high, as all knew, in his extempore sermons; he never had to prepare them. Now, as then, he was devoid of feeling. Stella had whitened, and turned away unsteadily. He did not trouble to watch her stumble downstairs and out to the street.

\*        \*        \*

Pilar heard her mistress come home. She was told to send for the child Sabrina. Thereafter she heard Sabrina receive the worst whipping of her life till she was thrust from the room, howling. 'I will see nobody,' said Stella. 'We are going to London. Pack my things and be ready to come for a day or two. Be quick; I won't wait.'

Pilar asked if any message was to be left for Sir Gareth if he should arrive. 'Say I've been taken ill, and must see a doctor,' Stella said. She had remembered the name of Towne of Lisson Grove.

# CHAPTER SEVEN

Stella and Pilar travelled up to London by train, and spent the night at a small little-known hotel in the Marylebone Road. It was not particularly clean, and there were fleas. Pilar complained while Stella lay on the bed. They arranged to settle and leave the next day, after the appointment arranged with Mr Towne.

His surgery proved not very alluring either. It was to be found between the grimy furtive houses in the district where young girls in trouble had long been brought either to bear their unwanted babies secretly, or lose them. 'Wait here in the carriage,' Stella told Pilar; they had taken a hackney. Stella got out; she was veiled, and carried enough money in her reticule. The man had to be paid in advance.

Pilar waited in some trepidation; she'd rather have gone in with her ladyship. After about an hour Stella appeared, almost hustled out of the door by a grimy attendant with blood on his coat. The cab-driver held the door open, and Stella entered and then collapsed. 'Let me lie up on the seat,' she said to a horrified Pilar. 'I think I'm still bleeding. They wouldn't let me wait.'

Pilar undid her own petticoat, which fastened at the waist, and padded Stella with it while she lay along the seat. Pilar sat then at her feet, chafing them. 'I want to go home,' Stella said, like a child. She had begun to shiver.

'Would it not be best to wait overnight at a more pleasant hotel? Tell him to drive into town, and I'll see to it.' She knew there must be better places to stay; it wouldn't be difficult. However Stella insisted that she wanted to go home to Leys.

They drove to Euston, and caught a train. Stella seemed a little calmer, and lay with her eyes closed; they'd reserved a compartment. Pilar had sent a telegram for Stevens to meet them with the carriage, and it was waiting; she'd never expected to be as glad to see his rat's face. He helped both women in without expression; the carriage started and jogged its way to Leys. Once there, Pilar aided her mistress upstairs, undressed her and put her to bed. 'I've told 'em to bring a hot brick,' was all she said. When it came she put it at Stella's feet. They were cold.

Pilar slept on the pallet that night, and by morning Stella was feverish, her cheeks burning with two bright patches of crimson. Soon she began to babble and toss about, and Pilar sent for Gareth from Ireland. It didn't matter what he thought; he should be there. Stella began to keep saying his name, asking when he would be with her.

'He is on the way by now, darling.' All her

envy and contempt had gone; this, once more, was beautiful Miss Stella, whose frilly petticoats she'd ironed gladly in Dublin, who must not die. If Gareth came in time, he would save her.

He would not be in time. The crossing must be delayed. Pilar knew, when Stella's hands, which she was holding, began again to grow cold. She was dead two hours before Gareth arrived.

He stood looking down on Stella's dead face. He would never know other than that she had died of a sudden fever. Pilar had withdrawn to the next room, leaving him alone with the body of his wife. She could hear the whispered agony of his grief.

'Stella. Stella. Oh, my love, my darling. Oh, my star. How shall I live? What is to become o me now? I should never have left you. Stella, Stella, I should never have gone away.'

Pilar could think of only one thing to do. It was night by then, but she went and fetched the child Sabrina from her cot and thrust her, sleepy-eyed, into his arms. She wasn't his, only the image of her mother; except for the eyes, it'd remind him of her. At the door of the death-chamber the fair curls shone, echoing those of the dead woman. Sabrina's feet were bare; there hadn't been time to find her slippers, to think of anything but to use her to comfort the stricken man who thought he was her father.

It was successful, as far as that went. After a pause Gareth seized the small warm bundle and began kissing and caressing it, stroking Sabrina's curls, sobbing over her like a woman. He kept her with him all night, perched on his knees, later clutched against him in bed. She was a living warm thing, like a little animal. He had forgotten she was deaf, and talked to her in a low voice, as though she had been Stella. That's what she'll be to him from now on, Pilar thought sourly; Stella. It's as well he isn't always at home.

In the morning they came, the doctor and the undertakers. It was assumed Lady Seaborne had died of a common fever; not much was asked. 'We won't bury her in that vault,' said Gareth suddenly, looking from above Sabrina's shining head. 'There is this new cremation. I can take her ashes with me to Ireland and scatter them at Raheere. That way she will be always with me.'

That makes two ways, thought Pilar. It was arranged.


CHAPTER EIGHT


Gareth had indicated to the town council that he did not require any official presence at the cremation, and he was angered, after all, to see the small prim figure of the chemist, then the

137

dark-clad one of the sheriff, emerge from a carriage at Woking. This was the first place in England free of controversy on the matter, and Gareth himself had given much agonised thought as to whether he could best endure the thought of Stella's body devoured at once by flame, or slowly by worms in the earth. Neither were tolerable, but her ashes at least could remain with him. He stood holding little Sabrina by the hand, giving him strength as the smoke from the chimney rose. No one else had come with him, by his own request; Pilar, Hannah and Brian Laracor waited in the mourning-carriage. Sabrina brought strength, almost consolation. He had no doubt she was sad at losing her mother. If he had known, Sabrina was not sad at all, but her child's face, as had been necessary all her life till now, showed no expression. The chemist remained by himself. The sheriff came over and stood near Gareth, overtopping him. His face was pale and exalted, as when he delivered his sermons.

'You have committed a sin against the Almighty. The bones of the dead are to rise at the last judgment. How can your wife's be among them if they exist no more? She must be counted among the damned, who will not see eternal life.'

In his eyes was a gleam of pale triumph. He bent towards Sabrina and laid his hand on her curls. 'Good day, young lady.'

She raised her head and surveyed him with his own cold eyes. Gareth had turned away, resisting a desire to smash Stern's face in. Later, he was given Stella's warm ashes. Later still, scattering them at Raheere, he told himself that every flower that bloomed, each blade of grass that grew, each primrose, would contain something of her.

*     *     *

He would return to Leys more frequently than of late years; he liked to pet, kiss and cuddle Sabrina. She must not, he had decided, grow up lacking either parent; he would be a mother and a father to her. When he was at home he liked to give her her bath at nights, rolling up his shirt-sleeves and plunging his arms into the warm soapy water where her little body sat. He came to know all of it, watching it grow like a flower. She had a skin like a white peach, like Stella's; hair like Stella's, little starry active hands, small shapely feet with nails like pink shells. She was a cherub who would grow into an angel, like her mother. When he had leisure he liked to keep her in his lap all day, playing with her; besides helping her to learn to read, he tried to teach her words by lips and tongue; but she had been so severely used for trying earlier that he had no success, and in the end left her to her silences. Books, he decided, must become her pleasure, as she would never

139

hear music; he bought her some with pictures of animals with their names below, cat, dog, monkey, elephant. As for Sabrina's writing, it remained a scrawl. He would kiss her a great deal, reward her with a sweetmeat put in her mouth when she had done well, but only a frown if she had done badly. Having been accustomed to sterner usage from everyone but Pilar and Stevens, Sabrina was content, but grew lazy. The episode of the doll, now long gone to its reward, was forgotten. Sabrina didn't seem to miss it. Gareth wanted to give her a puppy, but she was indifferent, and for the puppy's sake Gareth gave it instead to Brian Laracor, who taught it to walk to heel in correct fashion.

Otherwise Gareth did not pay much attention to his son. There was a tutor, a pony, school. Gareth deliberately thought of Brian's mother as Stella, who was dead. It was the way he had disciplined himself; the fact that he had had to be unfaithful to Stella was thrust down in his mind; it hadn't happened.

Pilar alone remembered that it had. Hannah died of a constriction of the bowels soon after Stella, and only Stevens the coachman and his mother up in town were left to remember the old days.

Pilar not only remembered, but noticed; not much escaped her. Sir Gareth would pet Miss Sabrina till she became a spoilt little monkey as soon as he'd gone, but she learnt then, quickly enough, that trouble didn't pay.

\*      \*      \*

Sabrina couldn't tell Gareth, whom she called Papa as it was easy to see by the lips, much. She certainly couldn't tell him she hadn't been sad in the least when Mama died; on the contrary, she was pleased. She knew enough to know this would shock him, and that it would not be to her advantage to do so. She thought him handsome, and liked to be close to him. As she grew older there began to be names put on labels for her to see and read. One was MRS STEVENS.

This personage had been Sir Eldred's housekeeper, and more, and the coachman was, of course, her son. That was all Sabrina knew except that Stevens looked like a rat, but he couldn't help it. He used to stroke and kiss her just like Papa, and when she'd been whipped he would soothe the sore place beneath her skirts.

That was until something happened. It was when she was older, and didn't go as often to hide in the old gilded coach. For one thing, Mama wasn't there any more, and when Pilar reproved her it was only with a wagged finger. Sabrina couldn't know about things like right and wrong, or anything except what could be touched, seen, smelt. She liked bright colours and shining things. Perhaps for that reason she went down to the old coach again one day and climbed in to look at the red velvet. It was quite old, and beginning to have bald patches and smell of mould. Sabrina, to make up for not being able to hear or speak, had a strong sense of smell, in the same way as blind people acquire an extra sense of touch. Papa must have told her that, probably through books.

She saw Stevens come in and knew he'd seen her arrive. He smiled and came to join her in the coach, which meant she couldn't get out again till he'd gone; the coach stood against the wall and you could only open the doors on one side. Stevens began kissing and stroking her as he always had, then playing the game they'd used to do together, with the things men grew as part of them and girls didn't. By now, Sabrina didn't like the game much and wanted to get away. Suddenly Stevens began to do something else. It went on for quite a long time, and hurt. Sabrina struggled and as soon as she could, ran off, pulling down her skirts. She decided not to go back to the coach any more. There was no way of telling anybody what had happened.

At the time she was not quite eleven years old. Stevens stood staring after her, surprised at himself. He hadn't meant to go as far with little Miss quite yet. Something had come over him.

She probably wouldn't come back now of her own accord. He decided to get his mother to help him. He didn't want to finish with Miss Sabrina; he wanted to go on much further, right up. You could tell already what she would turn into, given a bit of breaking-in; a hot little piece, like her mother.

\*　　　\*　　　\*

Mrs Stevens, who seemed smiling and pleasant, used sometimes to come down and take tea with Pilar, likewise Hannah before the latter died. Mrs Stevens, had Sabrina known, considered herself a cut above them both. The late baronet had shown his appreciation of her varied services by a legacy which had enabled her to keep a small house up in town. She was able to bring any gossip there was, which wasn't much these days since the sheriff took a blockage in his innards and wasn't as often seen. Mrs Stevens was even enabled to employ a maid-of-all-work who came in every day, and to have her son with her on his free time off. Her maternal feelings had from the beginning overcome his appearance.

\*　　　\*　　　\*

Once, Sabrina was somehow told, Papa had gone to Australia. It was to be for three years, a very long time. Laracor Industries were growing so successful now that a branch was to be opened in Melbourne. Gareth, to try to forget the aching lack of Stella, had agreed to go out himself and establish it, at the same time continuing to write for the paper. He had, of course, said farewell to Sabrina with a great many kisses, and promised to write with drawings of what Australia was like.

He did so, but the child missed him, and kind Mrs Stevens said to Pilar that the little dear might enjoy staying a night at the town house now and again; it made a change.

\*     \*     \*

Sabrina was driven up to the town's street with Pilar in attendance, then handed in to Mrs Stevens at her house. Pilar stayed for a cup of tea, then left in the carriage. Sabrina was shown the glories of the small town house; there were a great many crocheted mats covering everything. The maid must be kept busy ironing them. There was china behind a glass-paned cabinet, but it never came out. There was a plant in a brass pot, set by itself on an ugly dark green chenille tablecloth. There was a coal-scuttle made of brass as well, which the maid filled and kept polished. There was a teapot like a Toby jug, and a mourning souvenir of the long-dead Princess Charlotte, with her sorrowing widower prostrating himself below her fair, sculptured head. He was king of the Belgians by now, and quite old. Sabrina was beginning to pick up a certain amount from the newspapers, which Papa had said she was to be permitted to read. Most of what they contained bored her, but she looked at the engravings.

There was only one bed in the house, so she must be supposed to share it with Mrs Stevens. It was a large old four-poster with a counterpane crocheted in squares. This was carefully folded away after supper, which had been extremely filling, so much so that Sabrina felt drowsy. She was undressed and soon went to sleep, then woke up later although it was still dark, with the bed-curtains closed. Mrs Stevens had come into bed, smelling strongly of the stables. Strong hands grasped Sabrina, strong legs gripped hers. Something was being put up her after that, like it had been that earlier time in the old gilded carriage, with its musty smells of rotting velvet and old damp.

Sabrina gave her rare, harsh cry, but the sheet was stuffed in her mouth. She couldn't hear a man's voice saying, 'Shut up, you little bitch. You'll get to like it.'

In the morning there was Mrs Stevens, lying in the bed in her nightcap, smiling and visibly asking if Miss Sabrina had slept well. It might all have been a bad dream except for the stable smell, which lingered. Again, there was nobody she could tell.

\*         \*         \*

She didn't want to come back and stay at the town house any more after that, but was made to. Otherwise Pilar would have scolded her for being disobedient, making it clear from the usual wagged finger what she meant.

*       *       *

Pilar had no idea that anything of the kind was going on. After several visits the girl seemed less unwilling and sullen. She was at a difficult age, beginning to grow little swollen nipples. Pilar was aware of Mrs Stevens' previous reputation, but with Sir Eldred it must have been unavoidable; she had after all caused no scandal since, and seemed devoted to her son. It was not till the ineffable Mrs Comstock, who had been up very early owing to an unwonted indulgence in oysters, happened to look out of her window to see Stevens coming out of his mother's house fastening himself, and throwing something in the gutter before making off, and, knowing Miss Sabrina was visiting there, came immediately to tell Pilar, that suspicion grew. There wasn't anybody living there but his mother in the ordinary way. The maid didn't come in as early.

Pilar didn't waste time questioning a deaf girl. She made Sabrina lie down and carried out a certain examination with her finger. The child had been tampered with, frequently at that. She left her in strict charge of the

146

servants, and herself walked up the hill; she wasn't going to ask Stevens to drive her. The wind was strong, and blew against Pilar, causing her to clutch at her cloak. When had that happened to her before? She remembered; it didn't matter now. What had lately been done to young Sabrina was more important.

She knocked at the door of Mrs Stevens' house at last, went in and confronted that lady, who bridled but denied nothing.

'What's the harm? Nothing else'll happen to her, being the way she is. Jack sees to it he wears his condom. He's entitled to a bit of pleasure, he's on his own always, and he's taken a fancy to her. No, I won't tell him to stop; tell him yourself.' She added that she could say a thing or two about what Stevens had seen through the crack of the correction-house side door, when her late ladyship had been supposed to be taking an interest in the orphans. 'None of 'em ever thinks of who's driven them to places, or that they has eyes in their heads. What Jack saw happen as often gave him ideas of his own, I don't doubt. He saw enough of what the mother could do to want the daughter. Sabrina's got so's she doesn't mind, I dare say. It'll be someone else with her soon, if it isn't him.'

Pilar turned and walked out. She walked fast back to Leys, as the wind by now was with her. She did not enter the house, but went straight to the stables and the coach-house. The great old coach that had belonged to Sir Eldred reared in the shadows behind the horse-boxes, and there was somebody inside: two people. Pilar beheld the door, which was open, and the jerking buttocks of Stevens himself, with Miss Sabrina lying beneath him, skirts up and legs apart. Her eyes were closed and she was smiling. She'd got to like it, as Mrs Stevens had prophesied. She must have come to the stables of her own free will.

Pilar took a horsewhip down from the wall; the stable served as its own tack-room. She then brought the full weight of the whip down on Stevens' buttocks, so that he withdrew screaming. Pilar dragged him out by the scruff of his neck, shot a free fist into one of his eyes and blackened it, then as he stood staggering, breeches down, kicked him in the groin. He doubled up with pain, sobbing like a woman, and Pilar began to lay about him with the whip, catching him with the backlash as well. Sabrina had meantime curled up like a cat in the back seat of the carriage, watching enjoyably, with her strange eyes, through the opened coach door. Stevens, screaming obscenities, was by now on the floor; Pilar whipped mercilessly on. 'Get out,' she said at last to the whimpering bundle that had been a man. 'Don't show your rat's face here again.'

He left at once, as she found afterwards. For a time she was afraid he might be lying in wait, or that there might be talk in the town. There seemed to be none; Mrs Comstock, as usual, kept her counsel. Mrs Stevens' house proved to be empty and word spread that she had gone abroad, with her son, to Canada. As for Sabrina, Pilar took her back to the house and for the first time, caned her. The girl must be made to know that what she'd been doing was wrong, and there was no other way of making her aware of it. The trouble was that Stevens might already have made her randy at twelve years old. She must certainly be taken into the charge of Sir Gareth; when he returned: it was no longer her, Pilar's, responsibility. He must be told what had happened, as gently as possible, lest it happen again.

## CHAPTER NINE

County gossip had long ceased about the family at Leys House. They didn't hunt, and that left very little conversation or much else in common. One had called, and left a card. There had been the annual invitation to the Lord Lieutenant's garden party, with pleasant exchanges, parasols on the lawn, and strawberries and cream in course of expected proceedings. Lady Seaborne and her two children would go by themselves as a rule, the squire being almost invariably in Ireland. His wife had undeniably remained very beautiful, though perhaps eventually running a trifle to fat. It was understood she had worked laudably for charities. The children were well-behaved, the boy handsome like his father, growing fast and answering correctly when addressed. He showed an interest in the hunt, and as soon as he was old enough appeared at the meet; that earned general approval.

As time passed, and following the death of his wife, it was felt that Sir Gareth might as well make over the Leys inheritance to his son. He himself, it was clear, took very little interest. When Brian Laracor finally appeared at the Hunt Ball, every young lady present began to set her cap at him; but he seemed a reserved young man. As for his sister, it was tragic that so beautiful a little creature should be a deaf-mute. She seemed, at most times, to have been trained to stand silent and still, like a doll. It was unfortunate, and there was very little other than the dancing in which she could take part, although it was certainly rewarding to look at her while she did that.

Gareth himself began to make arrangements to transfer Leys to his son when it might legally happen, namely when the boy came of age. His own interests centred more and more on the Irish industries and the Dublin newspaper. When he met the Leys county he had very little to say to them or they to him. Brian Laracor was ideally suited to the life, and after leaving Eton expressed an interest in estate management, though certainly not in Ireland. Gareth visited his lawyers, and made the required arrangements. It was, in many ways, a relief to be rid of the burden his great-uncle had imposed on him. Brian Laracor would have appealed to the old squire in a way he himself had never managed, or tried, to do. He left it there for the time, and returned to business and the imminent prospect of Australia.

## CHAPTER TEN

Nemesis by then had overtaken the high sheriff at last in the form of a growth gnawing at his vitals. It turned him by degrees into a shrunken and yellowish living corpse, then a dead one. The occasion was made the most of by the town, which, commendably aware of the late sheriff's benefits to it, organised a procession of all sections of the community, clad in deep mourning, to walk behind the hearse. This boasted six black horses each decorated with sable ostrich feathers and drawing, as slowly as was feasible to them, the coffin itself, beneath a black pall enlivened, at Mrs Yeoman's instruction and according to her fancy, by the words OUR DEAR BROTHER HEZEKIAH in small white chrysanthemums. The final result had taken up all the room there was. Civic symbols decorated the coffin's top. It was a far finer display than had been arranged for the late ir Eldred, as was felt by all to be proper.

Speeches at the subsequent burial, conventionally in earth to allow for the Last Judgment, were copious, though a great deal was naturally left unsaid. Later a plain obelisk in red Ionian marble, in memory of the sheriff's services, was erected in the market square, and only those ribald souls who thought of such things as a matter of course murmured that it resembled nothing more than a giant phallus and that that was no less than it should be.

The young squire, as Brian Laracor was beginning to be called as his father was still in Australia, walked among the civic dignitaries with head respectfully bent. Afterwards he went back to Leys and played cards somewhat condescendingly with Pilar, telling her how everybody, as he put it, had enjoyed themselves.

'It's a fact at funerals,' Pilar said, dealing her hand. 'If anyone wants to cry, they cry at a wedding. When's your own?'

However Brian Laracor, then and later, showed no inclination to marry. He was a self-contained young man who settled down otherwise into the traditional expected pattern, hunting with the local pack, asking the parson, duly promoted in the public's estimation now there was no Hezekiah to preach as the spirit moved him, twice yearly to dinner. Pilar sighed a little, it was a long time since Gareth had gone away. She continued to keep a firm eye on Sabrina.

## CHAPTER ELEVEN

Sir Gareth Seaborne returned from Australia at last, leaving a local manager in charge. He was brown with the sun, but looked older, with lines engraved from nose to mouth, and hair which, though not by any means thinning, had turned silver at the temples by now. He was a handsome and, in all ways, a distinguished man. Sabrina flung herself at him, covering his face with kisses and perching on his knee as she had been used to do before he left.

Now, though, it was different. 'My girl has grown very beautiful,' he said sadly, seeing her mother in her. As she sat in his lap he absently lifted her little breasts where they lay beneath the gown. Sabrina moved her long slender limbs pleasurably. Pilar, watching, wondered if he'd had women in Australia; surely there could not have been as long spent in entire faithfulness to the memory of Stella? He must have been eagerly sought after in Melbourne circles, the mothers there being understandably anxious to settle their daughters with a titled widower, possessing looks at that, and whose import business appeared to be thriving.

However he had evidently not been interested enough, if so, to remarry. That was all Pilar decided she would ever know. As for that little monkey Sabrina, she ought to leave him alone; to her, he was one more man. There was a devil there, induced by Stevens: and Sir Gareth was fair game. Should he be warned Sabrina was not his daughter? Pilar decided against it. It was cruel to tarnish the memory of Gareth's dead wife. If he cared to see her again in Sabrina, what affair was it of hers, plain Pilar the housekeeper? She had done her duty as far as she saw it; now, she ought to desist, hard as it was. Still fondling Sabrina, Gareth told her he meant to take the girl back with him to Ireland, to Mrs Duveen. 'She has reared five daughters, and they all have practical skills,' he said, smiling. 'There is no reason why Sabrina should not learn from her, as well as having the two young women for company.'

He told Pilar one other thing; when on a visit to the outback, watching the rounding up of many hundreds of sheep for shearing, he had met the young man named Henry Yeoman, who had hired himself out to help the farmer. 'I noticed the late sheriff's double riding a horse as well as a barbarian would have done,' Gareth told her, 'and asked his name. To watch him with the sheep was an education. I should say he'd get on in life whatever he turned his hand to.' They hadn't talked much, he admitted, as he himself couldn't even yet understand broad Stry: and his own visit had been a short one made out of interest, at the invitation of a customer who bought Irish lace for his wife, back at the homestead. 'Everything's different out there, rougher, clearer. It's perhaps like England used to be when people had to contrive for themselves.'

Pilar took the opportunity to tell Gareth about the man Stevens' behaviour to Sabrina when he asked why there was a new coachman. He was horrified. 'The poor child,' he said. 'There are those with no conscience. You did right to get rid of the scoundrel.' Pilar didn't say how she had managed it; he had enough to disturb him already.

He continued to treat Sabrina carefully, as though she were porcelain; as he had latterly treated Stella, Pilar told herself grimly. Soon it was time for them to return across the water. By then, Pilar had got the girl ready with dresses, bonnets and cloaks for dry and wet weather, white cotton stockings and four pairs of shoes. She saw them off with a mixture of relief and sadness; Sir Gareth had Sabrina in charge, which was a relief: but he'd gone away. There was no real need for him to return now Brian Laracor was coming into his own;

shortly there would be the formal coming-of-age of the young squire, with speeches and bonfires and a traditional roast pig or two from the farms, turning on the spit in the fragrant night. It was a custom dating from Tudor times, when the first house had been built from the stones of the rifled abbey. She would have had to keep Miss Sabrina close by on such a night. It was as well she'd gone.


## CHAPTER TWELVE

By then, she was back.

Mrs Duveen, whose hotel was deservedly beginning to be a regular success, agreed with Gareth that it would be a good idea for Miss Sabrina to learn to cook. 'It's not likely she will ever have to,' as she put it, but it would be better than sitting about all day looking at pictures in the papers, or staring at her own reflection in the glass and combing out her long hair time and again.

Gareth was grateful. He hadn't time to have Sabrina with him constantly, between the noise of rolling machinery and the printing soot that lodged beneath one's fingernails. He bought the girl a linen apron from Laracor Industries and handed her over to Mrs Duveen and her daughters Grace and Martha, who, like their married sisters, had been taught early and

156

well.

Sabrina proved not a bad pupil, and in time could pound the rising dough, scramble eggs and baste roasting meat, and even by the end turn out a reasonable omelette or soufflé. Unluckily by then Idle Tom, the son his mother had always known would never stay out in Australia, came home. He'd borrowed the fare from Johnny, his brother, who had married and set up in the tea-importing business. Johnny's wife's parents had been convicts, Tom said, but it was never to be mentioned, and the household was so respectable you'd freeze. He'd tried the gold-fields, but had no luck; he never would have any, nor would any woman he married. He decided he would rather come home and go back, after all, to the farm. He did so, but his brothers and their wives had no time for anyone as lazy, and back again he came to Duveen's Hotel, and especially to the kitchen.

Gareth was confronted one day by Mrs Duveen at his office, propelling Sabrina in her cloak and bonnet. Mrs Duveen's handsome face was set. 'She's best at home,' she said firmly. 'I'll go across with her myself.' She would say no more, and Sabrina flung her arms round Gareth's neck as if for protection.

Gareth decided that at that rate it was best for her to go, whatever had happened. He paid her fare and Mrs Duveen's return one, and thanked her for her trouble in sparing the time to take the boat and the journey. No doubt she would say more to Pilar; and he himself could not forever expect the luxury of being able to stare in wonder at Sabrina's golden hair at the day's end, pretending to himself she was Stella.

*       *       *

Pilar and Mrs Duveen confronted one another at last. Sabrina was sullen; she hadn't wanted to come back to strict Leys. The young man who was Mrs Duveen's son had had handsome dark eyes, and admired her. Sabrina liked to be admired. She liked other things that followed admiration. There was no need for Mrs Duveen to have taken a hefty wooden spoon to beat her son out of the kitchen where she, Sabrina, had happened to be alone earlier at the stove. It had turned out the way things were sometimes, and made the day more interesting. She saw Mrs Duveen's lips move beneath her pork-pie hat as she talked to Pilar, and Pilar as usual looking angry.

'She needs an eye kept all the time, being the way she is. It wasn't her fault; she wouldn't know to beware of him. I've sent him off to find himself work; that's the answer,' had said the good lady, who wouldn't stay the night as she had to get back.

From what she told Pilar, it ought to be an occasion for the birch. It was, again, the only way the erring young woman would learn: but

Pilar restrained herself.

* * *

Sabrina was accordingly at home after all for the young squire's coming-of-age, and went out to the home field with Pilar in close attendance. After the speeches, which she couldn't hear, and seeing Brian Laracor's figure outlined against lit bonfires as the centre of attention, Sabrina joined hands with the tenantry in a round-and-round dance encircling the fires, over which they later jumped in pairs. Sabrina's partner was a reliable young man from the home farm, who could be trusted to behave himself with her; but it was exhilarating to be lifted by the waist and to leap with him over the fire. 'Wish,' she saw his lips say, but she didn't know what to wish for. She supposed she had everything she wanted, except Papa; when would he come home?

* * *

Gareth found that work had lost its savour once Sabrina had gone. Mrs Duveen returned and said the girl had been safely delivered to Pilar, who had her room ready. Gareth thought constantly of what Sabrina's life must be now; walking in the garden, feeding the peacocks and waterfowl, sitting idly about the house if there was nothing to read that interested her, or if it was raining. Her only real faculty was her sight. To know more of the wider world would benefit her, give her more to remember than she had now. She might live to be old, or not; and he had lost Stella without spending enough time in her company. The same thing must not happen again.

About then, old Dan O'Toole died at Raheere. He had given no signs of being ill or of having a weak heart. He was simply found dead in his armchair when the servant came in, having sat in it from the night before. No doubt this was as good a way to go as any, but it lessened the number of people who remembered Stella and could speak of her.

It also meant that the former factor's house was vacant. Gareth gave up his room at the hotel, knowing he would miss the excellent food, and moved back meantime, trying to interest himself again in the shoemaking and weaving. A couple occupied the Dublin house and the husband made an adequate editor. Gareth himself was not much missed, truth to tell; he admitted it, looking at himself in his shaving-mirror and seeing a man whose youth had left him long ago.

'The room's yours again any time you need it,' Mrs Duveen had said. She'd grown very fond of the quiet gentleman, never troublesome the way some were. He'd spent his evenings writing, writing his articles; from the street you could see his shadow on the blind, quill in hand. He didn't deserve such a daughter, too good at pulling up her skirt for whoever came.

If she had known, Gareth was already arranging to take Sabrina on the equivalent of the Grand Tour; Spain, Italy, France and Switzerland. She should feast her eyes on great paintings and glorious mountains topped with snow beneath the stars, and remember them always. It was his gift to her, for reminding him of Stella.

# Part Three

# CHAPTER ONE

If babies can remember—and memory goes further back than anyone thinks—Brian Laracor had reason for knowing himself unloved. His father did his duty by him and sent him to Eton, where at least he was able to meet other chaps who felt as he did in general about the way life ought to be lived; in an orderly fashion, with no deaf-mute sisters, no beautiful mothers going off on charity-errands and returning flushed, dishevelled and vague, no absent fathers in places like Ireland, editing the wrong kind of newspaper, pointedly refraining from the things Brian liked to do, such as hunting. He took pride in the fact that at his first time out, he was in at the death and was blooded on the cheek with the fox's brush. Nobody at home was interested.

He was also embarrassed by the servant Pilar in some way he could not define. Servants didn't have feelings one need consider, and Pilar had certainly never made hers troublesome: yet he felt that she made some demand on him he couldn't understand, let alone fulfil. He treated her distantly, along with the other servants, got on with his own life and made his own friends. They were of his own way of thinking, met with at Eton, trained in traditional values, averse to matters such as labour rights and equality for all, socialist views and disturbance of the established order. The established order was unique, and worth preserving. He himself would do what he could in terms of the care of the estate and its farms, which he began to supervise carefully. He was interested in bloodstock and in cattle-breeding, and would be seen as a matter of course at the local agricultural show. Once he proudly led round his own bull, which had won a rosette. He was on nodding terms with the local farmers, while still expecting them to raise their caps to him except at the meet; he was, after all, following his coming-of-age, the squire of Leys.

He was flattered when he was at last approached with a request that he stand as Member for the borough. This office had formerly been filled by a moribund scion of a race much older than that of Sir Posthumus, and to supersede him would have been unthinkable. When he died, the shops closed and black hoods were put on the old gentleman's heraldic stone eagles, one on either side of the gateway to his mansion some miles off. They were a legacy from the building of the original castle on the site, which in its time had disturbed an eagle's nest. The remains of the castle reared at the back of the subsequent mansion, built somewhat earlier than Leys House. Brian Laracor had dined there once or twice. Evidently the old boy, on his deathbed, had recommended him as a sound young man who wouldn't fail to toe the party line if elected. There were certain elements in the borough nowadays, especially in Leys itself, which would disturb the state of things profoundly if allowed to have their head. It was no doubt a legacy from the long-ago days when subjects had executed a king. Since then there had, of course, been a switching of allegiances, but all of that went up to establish the traditional Englishman; and nobody, by then, was more traditional than Brian Laracor, fortified by a built-in suspicion of anything at all unusual. The rival candidate, a man named Noakes, need not be considered in a safe seat and could revert, after the election, to his traditional occupation of watchmaker, in his shop in the High Street.

Meantime there was electoral mayhem of the usual kind, which even invaded Leys. Representatives of officialdom came and went, Brian was asked to make speeches to the constituents, which he managed to do by dint of the usual expedient of saying nothing at all and taking a long time to say it. He likewise had to do things which by nature he would have avoided, such as charming the townspeople's hopeful wives and kissing their sticky children. As he was young, handsome and unmarried it was on the whole not too difficult, except that he didn't really like children in the least. He had assumed that in proper course, he would be expected to marry and produce them, but had put off the event as long as possible. Like the deceased High Sheriff he valued his privacy, and a wife would invade this in the nature of things. The selection committee would have preferred him at least to be spoken for, but Brian Laracor found it impossible even to pretend a personal interest he could not feel. After all, as he put it to them, Pitt the Younger had contrived a political career of some distinction from the frozen heights of his chosen bachelor solitude.

'Solitude with a bottle,' one unbridled voter shouted from the back of the hall, but was quickly dealt with and the situation was not allowed to recur. Very few, by now, knew in any case who Pitt the Younger had been. All they wanted was to go on living in peace after the election. Noakes was making inflammatory statements about trade unions, and hadn't a hope; such persons were pirate ships that passed in the night, and to presume to oppose the squire was in any case an impertinence.

To Brian Laracor's extreme embarrassment and somewhat relief, Noakes was elected by a small majority who favoured the good old moral laws of Cromwell's England and remembered the whisperings there had been from time to time about this young squire's late mother, though nobody by now could be certain. What was bred in the bone would out, perhaps. It was time for a change anyway.

Brian Laracor took his defeat as a gentleman should and appeared, unruffled, at the next meet, with not a hair out of place beneath his black velvet hunting-cap and a secret song in his heart that, having done what was expected of him, it hadn't been his fault if the matter had not come to any foreseeable conclusion. Times were changing, and he didn't want to know any more. He would continue as he always had. He was, by then, twenty-five.

## CHAPTER TWO

To Mrs Yeoman's mortification, a stocky young male with the bow legs of Genghis Khan, otherwise closely resembling her late brother the sheriff, strode into the correction-house one day and said, 'You must be my old woman.' Nothing else he said was intelligible. He kissed her on both cheeks. The orphans, whether sewing or sweeping, looked towards him with one accord like flowers towards the sun.

That was the beginning of it. Henry said he'd made enough money—he called it something else—to visit the old country, and herself, for quite some time. He handed her a black leather case in which reposed a large pink opal he'd dug himself. It was the most beautiful thing she had ever possessed, and

169

tears began to course down her cheeks. 'That's dinkum,' said Henry. He then sat down and ate a large meal.

His mother—she wasn't ashamed of it now—put the opal away, and often looked at it in secret. It was supposed to be bad luck to wear them, but surely it was all right just to look. Nothing else about Henry could remain secret in any case: unlike his uncle, he always spoke about what he did or intended. Nevertheless as most of what he said was in broad Stry, it might as well have remained unsaid and unsung. Whether intelligibly or not, what he tried to tell his mother was that he'd taken up with a man called Cornwall, they'd gone to the outback where you had to sleep behind a stockade because if you didn't you would never wake up and would be found at some time later on with a spear in your back, and they'd founded a stud farm near the Beaufort River. He'd kept a share in that and it was doing well, because out there, with the races and the rounding up of sheep, everyone needed horses, even for carriage-driving to keep up your end in Van Diemen's Land.

As well, Henry had panned for gold and, unlike Idle Duveen, had had luck more than once. He'd invested in property at Kalgoorlie because in years to come, they'd still hope to find gold there and would want somewhere to shack up. No, he'd never married and probably never would, because women talked too much.

He had other idiosyncrasies. He always kept a paraffin matchbox in his left hand, from habit; if you lost them in the outback or on the goldfields, you hadn't any. This showed prudence and foresight, and Mrs Yeoman was increasingly proud of him. He gave her money and bought beer for all the orphans, who fell about for some time.

Life had altogether expanded for Mrs Yeoman; she had cast her bread on the waters and it had returned after many days, just as Hezekiah would have put it himself. She found she had largely forgotten Hezekiah. The light shone on the rainbow aspects of her secret opal, and she began to rejoice in her no longer secret son. She walked down the town's main street on Henry's arm, in her best bonnet, bowing and smiling to right and left. Everyone said how like the late sheriff Henry was and what a comfort he must be to her.

He was evidently prepared to stay for some time, but not for ever. She didn't think she herself would venture out to Australia again at her age. This was a pleasant interlude, to be made the very most of. Mrs Yeoman made the most of it while it lasted. So did the orphans. Future apprenticeship stakes were booming, but one didn't think in those terms. Henry was still distinguished by his bushman's hat.

\*       \*       \*

As a rule Pilar was content with her own company, but now and again she would have herself driven to take tea with Mrs Comstock and Mrs Yeoman, whose respective duties lay more lightly upon them both since the sheriff's death. Mrs Yeoman in particular had a fondness for a certain kind of seed-cake, whose seeds inconveniently lodged themselves in her false teeth in the course of mastication. She would briefly excuse herself. This was an expected ritual, and while the good lady was out repairing the damage Mrs Comstock leaned across her teacup in triumphant confidence.

'Mrs Yeoman's son Henry is home from Australia. Don't say anything. He's the image of his uncle.' She implied that there had been havoc, now as then, wrought among the orphans, silly creatures.

'Does he mean to stay?' enquired Pilar politely. She didn't suppose it had remained a secret, but Abigail liked to make one out of everything.

'Not once he's got what he came for. They're all the same.'

This dark statement could not be elucidated further, because Mrs Yeoman, her porcelain duly rectified, came back into the room and poured herself a second cup of tea. The talk ran on everyday things, and enquiries were made as to Brian Laracor's health. 'You might almost be a mother to him,' remarked

Mrs Yeoman, who missed a great deal if it did not concern her. 'The squire himself is very seldom at home.'

They parted, and as she drove back Pilar beheld what could only be Henry Yeoman, walking unabashed down the street. If she had not been told of his coming she would have thought she was looking at a ghost, shorn of civic glory; the late sheriff himself, having shed several years and somehow donned a shako and brown shirt. Dressed like that, he looked approachable, but so had the sheriff been if you knew how. Henry Yeoman was striding along towards town, but Pilar didn't tell the coachman to stop. It was enough to know that such a young man existed. Abigail needn't have made such a fuss.

## CHAPTER THREE

Sabrina and Gareth had by that time taken ship from Belfast. Gareth saw to it that Sabrina had a cabin near his own; remembering Mrs Duveen's set face and the earlier episodes of Stevens, he kept a firm eye on any advances made, any glances cast at her; these were inevitable no matter where they went. She seemed happy enough to cling to him, and they walked the deck arm-in-arm; it was a smooth voyage for once.

He had decided that he would follow the course of his own travels in his youth, with Spain first; green Galicia, with its statues of St Lucy and her eyes on a dish; had that really happened? Haloes were spectacular, so were spectacles perched on statues in churches, a proof of aristocracy he couldn't explain to Sabrina. There would, however, be Granada, beautiful with its carvings from Morisco days, and the Generalife gardens heavy with roses. She would bend and smell those. Then there would be Madrid and the Prado, with its portraits of doomed and beautiful royal children with powdered hair she couldn't resist, and the unforgettable Goyas; crumbling Charles IV and his lascivious queen, seen naked as La Maja. Sabrina stared at that, and at Saturn swallowing his children. It was uncertain how far she could understand stories of which she had no knowledge simply by looking; she must read more, he decided, when they returned home. He explained as much as he could meantime in writing and sketches, then they toured Portugal, where the saints in the churches no longer wore spectacles. Sabrina was intrigued by the oval haloes, different from those in Spain. A Portuguese saint would be instantly recognisable in heaven. Also, the river was magnificent. They drank wine, she and Papa, and ate oranges fresh from the trees. They explored old monasteries, on entering which

Sabrina was requested to cover her hair. Otherwise Gareth could not help feasting his eyes on it, and at nights would brush it out for her, as he had been used to do for Stella. He began to feel increasingly as if Stella was with him. He had been lonely in Australia, lonely and sad in Dublin. Now and again, he sent articles to the *Tribune* from abroad.

They travelled on into Italy, staring at the Pyrenees with their crazy shapes, as though God had gone mad with a pair of scissors. There was so much he wished he could say to this girl with golden hair. 'There are no more Pyrenees' would never be explicable to her, because she would never understand the need for the Sun King's marriage to a stupid bride.

Italy was different. They travelled through the north towns, seeing the frescoes in the red-and-white churches, seeing Assisi, seeing Padua and Pisa and its leaning tower. They saw the incorrupt body of a little crooked saint who had been dead four centuries, had been blind all her life, and still cured blind children. Was there a saint who would cure the deaf? Could he, her father, ever hope that Sabrina would hear and speak? She was beauty itself to survey; perhaps after all there was contentment in silence. Wherever they went he would watch her enchanting face, upturned to survey one marvel after the next. She would remember, surely, some of them for the rest of her life. He continued to want it to be as full as possible. The intention grew in him as they travelled on, day after day.

Sabrina seemed to take in a great deal in Florence. Rome was too much for her, and she craned her neck up at Michelangelo's ceiling where some people had ordered linen draperies to be painted over the flying naked masterpieces. Then and later on, seeing the statue of David, undraped, she indulged in her harsh forbidden laughter. Otherwise there were too many statues, too much ruined splendour, too baroque a grandeur to be understood if one could do no more than see.

While still in Rome, Gareth tried to arrange painting lessons for her from a fashionable portrait-painter, staying present while Sabrina, in a blue smock, handled brushes and a palette uselessly. She had no talent, the painter admitted after a fortnight's sessions, but he would greatly like to paint her naked; would the signor permit?

Gareth promptly forbade it, and they left; but within his later recollection, as in hers, from Florence, was the Botticelli Venus, slender and golden-haired, borne in on her shell to shore at Cythera, created out of sea-foam or, as the older legends had it, from the last of the mutilated Uranus' outpoured seed as he flew off to eternal and outraged seclusion on his remote planet. Sabrina had stared at the painting for a long time, swinging her hips. He knew she remembered it, also the other of Venus with Mars, lying asleep in her lap; the murdered Giuliano de'Medici and his mistress Simonetta, her perfect breasts outlined by her narrow girdle. How like Stella both aspects of Venus were! The languor of the sleeping god's limbs expressed satiety.

There had been Rome, there had been Florence: thereafter they went on to Venice. Sabrina clapped her hands in delight at the widely inhabited water, the skimming gondolas, the striped poles at landing-places. This was much better, a place full of the life she had lacked till now.


## CHAPTER FOUR

Mrs Yeoman had lately taken what proved to be a mild seizure, and her son Henry asked Abigail Comstock to come in and lend her aid. He himself could neither read nor write, he never felt the need of either, and Abigail could see to the correction-house ledgers and whatever else had to be done. Having an enquiring nature she agreed instantly; she'd always wanted to know what went on up there, they didn't tell you everything.

Having seen Henry off on his evening pilgrimage to the local inn—he had a walk, she decided, just like his uncle's—she saw to poor Mrs Yeoman, helped her drink a cup of tea out

177

of a lopsided mouth, then betook herself to the desk where papers were. Mrs Yeoman had early asked for her opal, and held it in her good hand, staring down. Below it, in the desk, had been kept certain envelopes including her Will, a copy of which was also with the town's lawyer.

Abigail came on an envelope which said nothing on the outside and which was sealed. She was consumed with interest; this might be her only chance of finding out whatever it contained. She took it to the kettle, which still steamed, and held it till the flap was loose, then drew out the enclosed document. It was lengthy and in a spidery hand; her short-sighted eyes brightened with prurient interest as she recognised the old sheriff's fist. Slipping it into her reticule—she'd return it, of course, when she'd had a good read of it at home—she left an available orphan in charge of Mrs Yeoman, with strict instructions to inform herself or Mr Henry if anything more should go wrong.

Once at home, she settled down over another pot of tea and a good fire laid by the living-out servant. Abigail liked the place to herself at nights. To be unobserved, as now, was useful.

**To whom it may concern**
*This is the testament of me, Hezekiah Stern, aware as I am that my days are*

178

numbered. *I do not intend this document to be revealed until after the death of my sister, known as Mrs Yeoman. The full truth would kill her, although she is aware of a certain amount.*

*By my failure to speak I have defrauded the town of Leys of the legacy left them by the late Sir Eldred Seaborne. A certain sum was to become theirs on the failure of his successor and great-nephew, Sir Gareth, to produce a male heir within five years of his existing marriage.*

*Sir Gareth had no children by his wife. Few except myself know that he sired a son on the servant Pilar, who is still in residence at Leys House, and this child was passed off as the child of Lady Seaborne, who believed herself to be barren. I knew that this was unlikely and that the fault was a lack of husbandly decisiveness on the part of Sir Gareth. Most women need a master, and he gave in to her whims. Later I myself lay with her many times in fleshly lust, and early fathered a daughter on her who Sir Gareth was persuaded was his. This girl is deaf but in appearance resembles her mother.*

*Lady Seaborne later became importunate, said she was with child by me again, and I dismissed her as she was becoming an embarrassment to my civic position. I believe she then went to an*

179

*abortionist, became infected, and died. My daughter was brought up by her supposed father and by Pilar, who was strict with her; but a man named John Stevens, who has tried to blackmail me over the whole matter, says he has had carnal knowledge of her. I paid him to keep his other knowledge to himself provided he and his mother took themselves to Canada and did not return. He had evidently witnessed Lady Seaborne with myself on repeated occasions, and threatened to tell Sir Gareth. Unfortunately the latter had not taken his marital rights since my daughter's birth, which I believe was a difficult one. Stella would have been unlikely to be able to ensure that a second child was thought by him to be his.*

*Stevens evinced particular spite against the woman Pilar, who he said had attacked him with a whip on finding him with my young daughter. Had I informed him, which I did not, that Pilar is the young squire's mother he would in turn have informed the town council at once. It was best to get him out of the country, and I trust that I have merited certain points in my favour with the Almighty for doing so. Otherwise I have been guilty of many sins, the commonest of them being concupiscence. By the time this statement is found my bones will long have been bare of flesh and its temptations.*

*I should have liked to leave what I possess to my sister and to the town, but the payments to Stevens in Canada have left relatively little, except perhaps enough to bury me with some honour. When the payments cease, Stevens may well return and make trouble for my daughter. I do not want this, and hope that Providence will dispose otherwise. She appears to have my disposition, which together with her deafness may mean that she ends wretchedly. I enjoin whoever reads this to see that she is provided for.*

*(Signed and dated) Hezekiah Stern, Sheriff*

## CHAPTER FIVE

Sabrina had come in with her father to the old palazzo which was now an inn, following their evening walk along by the Grand Canal to watch the lights and gondolas, although Sabrina could not hear the singing. Gareth had gone to the taverna for a last glass of wine, but Sabrina wanted to undress; it had been a humid day. She reached her room, took off her petticoat and chemise, and her shoes and stockings, then sat naked before the glass to let down her long hair, which had developed from childhood fairness to a deep gold.

Its shining length reminded her of something; the painting in Florence of the Botticelli Venus. Sabrina knew she resembled her, the beautiful Simonetta Vespucci who had been the model for the portrait with the shell, also with Mars. Sabrina remembered the one with the shell best; Venus had been the only person in the portrait.

She began to play with her own abundant locks, trailing them across her body, knotting and twisting them like the painting. It wasn't possible really to have had hair as long as that; it would have got in the way when Simonetta walked. Sabrina amused herself, playing with her hair and watching the reflected ripples of water on the ceiling. The Grand Canal was just below, with all the life of Venice.

She was restless. Why wouldn't Papa make love? He caressed her, kissed her, brushed out her hair every night. When she was small he had used to give her her bath. He must know every part of her except one. Why wouldn't he be like Stevens and Tom? She would try to make him; tonight, when he came in to brush her hair, no doubt expecting to find her in her bed-gown as usual. She wouldn't be. She put up a hand and yawned; it was quite late, he wouldn't be long.

When he came in it was to perceive the goddess of love, hair knotted as in the painting, not long enough to disguise the part

Venus had kept hidden, poised on her shell. Exquisite pale thighs, slightly open, revealed the doorway to delight. He had drunk more than one glass of wine. The outcome was inevitable.

Gently, predictably, he entered her. This was Stella, until she opened her eyes. Their colour bewildered him for instants; this wasn't Stella, after all, but a stranger. He kissed them shut, then before leaving kissed whichever she was on the mouth. This was Stella again; yet within himself he knew it wasn't so, and that he must not compromise the goddess. He tried to persuade himself that it was his duty to teach Sabrina all a woman could feel; the experiences she'd had had been unpleasant. Then he told himself he was a hypocrite. He was already infatuated with her flesh, the pearly globes of breasts she'd grown. Her response had been like nothing he had ever imagined. He was filled with excitement and fulfilment. This had been intended by the gods. It should happen again, but he must buy Sabrina a mask to cover her disconcerting eyes when they made love.

There was a shop along one of the smaller canals. They would go there first thing tomorrow.

Sabrina felt triumph. She'd made Papa do it at last. He wasn't as good at it as Stevens, or Tom at the hotel. Perhaps he'd get better next time, and the next.

*     *     *

The innkeeper's wife, who had been watching at the keyhole—all of them had a mild curiosity concerning the handsome English milord and the exquisite young lady who called him Papa but otherwise could not speak—took her eye away. It was true; the mistress was his daughter, or his daughter was his mistress; it didn't matter which way round, it wasn't good for the name of the house. The *padrone* must be consulted; it was possible that they must be asked, with politeness, to leave tomorrow.

*     *     *

Sabrina and Gareth had gone out early, taking coffee at a *baracca* and walking on hand-in-hand along the narrow canal-side ways to the mask shop. Sabrina tried one after the other on with delight; she was exhilarated after the triumph of last night. Here were white masks with long noses, black ones rimmed with sparkling sequins, a large purple feathered one she would have liked to take home. However Papa made her put on a plain silver one, also bought her a little black Venetian tricorne hat and a rose-coloured domino, which covered all of her; it was what was worn here in the evenings. Then they took a gondola and went out to the islands and came back in the dusk, with all the lights gleaming though the stars were not yet out. *Sul'mare luccica, l'astro d'argento,* sang the boatman. It meant money even though there were as yet no stars. This couple, like all couples, made love. Gareth kissed Stella's mouth and none other, saw Stella's golden hair gleam between hat and upper veil; she could no longer stare with the eyes of a cool stranger, the mask hid them conveniently. Stella had always liked rose-colour. He remained prudent and gentle, however, he must by no means compromise her, this girl who had become Stella, except for her unseen eyes.

\* \* \*

On return to the palazzo, they were met by the *padrone* with their gear ready packed. There had been *incesta*, they were politely told; it was not the custom here.

They made ready to leave Venice. Gareth felt deep shame: but by now could not extricate himself. He hadn't slept with a woman since the time of Irish primroses, when Sabrina had been conceived. The gods had arranged it. He was helpless, their victim: and hers.

\* \* \*

As intended, a little later on, they took a coach

towards Switzerland, and stopped at an auberge high in the mountains. It began to snow, and continued thickly for four days. There was nothing to do but make love. With flakes falling thickly beyond the window, Gareth savoured repeatedly the yielding body of Aphrodite, nevertheless remaining prudent while feeling sinful. It was his nature in such ways; only on one occasion had he ever forgotten himself totally, and he would not permit his memory to retain that occasion.

Sabrina was growing bored, less remembering Stevens—he'd after all got at her slowly over a long time, and she'd been only a child—than the eager young man at the Dublin hotel whom Mrs Duveen had chased out with a wooden spoon. He'd shown signs, for the time that was given him, of becoming an interesting lover. The insatiable blood of the sheriff raced in Sabrina's veins, prudence was wasted on her, and she rejoiced in fornication; it was her only fulfilment. Every man she had ever seen, except Brian Laracor, wanted it with her, as she could tell; even that painter in Rome, who had shocked Papa with whatever it was he'd asked about. From the heart of her eternal silence, Sabrina knew certain things no one had ever told her. There was no need for speech, even hearing: only her looking-glass, a comb, and this. Papa would do for the time being. Sabrina thrust her young body at him hungrily, wishing he'd do it harder. Soon, there might perhaps be somebody better.

## CHAPTER SIX

At Interlaken, Gareth bought a ring and slipped it on Sabrina's fourth left finger; it discouraged stares. He also bought her a blue gown with white embroidery and a small carved angel playing a bass viol. They travelled on through the mountains to a valley inn with low eaves made of carved wood, where the climbers and skiers came down in the evenings, and there was music at that time. As Sabrina couldn't hear it, they would go out and walk under the stars, which seemed just below the high tops, with their lights from the upper villages. Coming back, Sabrina could still not hear the music, which was played by a dark-haired young man with a zither; he took parties climbing by day. Everyone looked at Sabrina with interest, and Gareth took her straight up to their room and lay with her.

He was beginning to be wretched, thinking of the return to England; how could this continue there? One solution would be to find Sabrina a husband who would promise not to touch her, and, himself, to continue as her lover. The web of deceit depressed him, but after all he'd lived with it for years; ever since having to qualify illegally for his great-uncle's legacy. The results were coming home to roost. He was a most guilty man.

He tried to forget it for the time, sleeping with Sabrina in his arms under the same quilt. The music still sounded below. They wouldn't disperse till late. He continued to fondle her breasts, gently.

One day Sabrina came down early after breakfast coffee. Papa—she mustn't call him that now, evidently—was shaving. The young man who played the zither at nights was cleaning his instrument; later he would go out with the climbers. He worked hard. He looked at her and smiled. 'Why do you never come down to listen and sing?' he asked in German; he could speak three languages and had Italian blood. This was the loveliest girl he had ever seen, and her old husband kept her to himself. The only opportunity was now.

Sabrina put her fingers in her ears and towards her mouth, indicating that she couldn't hear or speak. She saw the young man come towards her, and he took her by the wrist and led her behind the dais where he played in the evenings. What followed was pleasant. She pulled down her skirts eventually and went back, reluctantly, upstairs. Outside, skiers were beginning to appear, swift expert shapes against the snow. She stood watching out of the window for a time till Gareth was ready to take her for their walk along a part of the valley, where there was a waterfall in summer, frozen at this season.

## CHAPTER SEVEN

The incriminating paper Mrs Comstock had discovered remained in her reticule longer than she had intended. Having made herself aware of its contents, this was one more secret to be contained in her flat bosom alongside all the rest. She would have returned the paper whence it came, namely to the desk in the correction-house office. However fate intervened in the form of a second, and fatal, seizure for Mrs Yeoman, and in making arrangements with the undertakers Abigail not unnaturally forgot about the incriminating contents of her reticule. There the envelope stayed, while Henry sat grieving beside the corpse of his old woman, saying he'd only just discovered her in time, and she'd been dinkum. He insisted that the opal be buried with her; she'd seemed fond of it, and it was left between her clasped and helpless hands while the coffin was screwed shut. The undertaker, who had already cast a desirous eye on the shining stone, quietly unscrewed everything and helped himself to that, and her spurious wedding ring, after everyone had gone away. Nobody would ever know.

Meantime, with the orphans shuffling respectfully past the closed coffin, Abigail realised she couldn't leave them alone with Henry, even though he was announcing that after all this was over, he'd make tracks down under. In the meantime several apprentices might be conceived to assuage his grief, and she couldn't cope with it as Mrs Yeoman had continued manfully to do. In other words, she herself must in conscience stay here till a replacement was found: and meanwhile it had also occurred to her that the envelope, marked to be opened after Mrs Yeoman's death and addressed To Whom It May Concern, might perfectly well apply to her as much as to the next corner.

While Henry went out for a breath of air and to drown his sorrows for an hour or two, Abigail nipped back to her own abode to collect a few necessaries. On the way she had a chance encounter in the street. A rat-faced man, unshaven and looking decidedly like a tramp, was seated outside the public house. It could be nobody but Stevens, back for money or else to make trouble now the sheriff's Canadian payments had dried up.

Abigail knew she must immediately warn Pilar. She sent a quick note down to Leys House by the penny post, and said she would like a word, if possible before the funeral; it admitted of no delay; would Pilar come up in the carriage to the office as soon as she could?

She, Abigail, had something to show her.

*     *     *

Pilar had been taught, at the orphanage long ago, to cipher and read, but her skills had been allowed to rust. At sight of the spidery hand she asked Abigail to read it aloud to her, and the reading took place in the room where Mrs Yeoman's coffin still lay, a silent witness to past turpitudes.

'Well,' was all Pilar would say at the end, 'nothing surprises me.' She added that Sir Gareth ought perhaps to see it, or again perhaps not. She would have to think about it. He was away at present on the Continent with Miss Sabrina. 'Will you let me take charge of the letter?' she asked. Mrs Comstock, anxious to shed anything that looked like evidence of collusion, agreed. If it hadn't been for seeing that Stevens, she vouchsafed, she might have kept the whole thing to herself.

Perhaps so will I, thought Pilar. It would hurt Sir Gareth greatly; there seemed no immediate need for him to know the truth, except that Stevens might try blackmail, which meant he'd be told anyway. She would think about it as she'd said. She would wait. Stevens wouldn't be at all likely to come near her again, remembering last time. He might go to Sir Gareth, or even to the young squire. Pilar held her peace.

Soon, news came that they were on their way home. Sir Gareth and Miss Sabrina. They'd been to Switzerland and they'd been to Aix. Brian Laracor brought the information absently; he lacked imagination beyond the next covert.

## CHAPTER EIGHT

Travelling north, Gareth still remembered Switzerland. He could hardly forget; Sabrina snuggled against him in the coach, her enchanting face bordered in furs against the cold, her gloved hand in his, held on purpose against his thigh. He could by no means free himself of her in mind or body: since the day behind the frozen waterfall he had remained increasingly wretched, unable to see any end whatever to the situation; she had become his succuba, draining the life from him, yet by now he could not stop himself from invading her, attempting to possess her, no longer deluding himself that this was anyone but Sabrina. Stella had never clung to him with strong young legs, forcing him up her, dragging him down on the ledge behind the waterfall so that because of the cold, he had wrapped both of them in his cloak; and seeing her face wrapped in its dark folds, eyes closed, had begun to sob against her and utter Stella's name. Then he had seen Sabrina's grey-green eyes open and stare, not at himself but out to where, beyond the long pale pillars of frozen ice suspended as it were in mid-air, a party of climbers was ascending the snowy peaks. She was watching them, no longer aware of him lying within her. Their leader was the young man who played the zither in the evenings. She had forgotten him, Gareth, as if he no longer existed. The sensation of loneliness he felt struck deep.

They had left the canton in a day or two, driving up towards Germany; to take her to Vienna was pointless when she could hear no music, though he would have enjoyed parading her beauty at the Staatoper, where eligible young ladies showed themselves at the interval with a view to attracting eligible young men. Sabrina attracted men wherever she went. He forced himself to remain one of them, lying within her teasing, thwarting body every night; by now she might have been a lovely heartless puppet, with a part he knew he would never reach. Having captured him, like a mermaid with a drowning sailor, she would be uncaring that he was losing his identity, his life. He was nobody and nothing now but her ageing lover, no longer himself or anyone. He wept often against her, and her answer was to toy with his hair.

'Papa.' She knew she mustn't say it when there were other people present. She would say it, on purpose, when they were alone. She knew how it made him feel. It amused her.

At Aix, old Aachen, Gareth garnered some comfort. They stayed at a hotel whose breakfasts were in the German mode, ham, hard-boiled eggs, different kinds of *würst,* fruit, rye bread and fresh butter and plenty of milky coffee. Gareth left Sabrina pouring coffee for them both while he answered a telegram which had come for him at the hall porter's desk. It was from the *Tribune* and required an immediate answer. He sent it, then returned to find Sabrina being thumbed in some anticipation by a businessman from Berlin. 'Permit me, *mein Herr*', Gareth said coldly. The man bowed and went. The coffee by now was equally cold, and after breakfast Gareth fetched their cloaks and took Sabrina smartly out to the cathedral. He downed the thought that had unwittingly arisen that he was in charge of a little bitch in heat; the episode with the German hadn't been her fault. Wherever she went such things would happen if she was left alone.

The cathedral was still full of memories of the great emperor Charlemagne. His giant image, crowned in gold and with enamel eyes, had once filled the whole of the chapel as the emperor's person would have done in life. This was the man who had fashioned Europe. A guide accosted them, talking by request in bad English, and dwelt appreciatively on the number of the emperor's wives rather than his conquests, also the excessive love the great conqueror had for his daughters. 'He would permit none of them to marry, but kept them in his palace behind a *Staket*, a stockade, and would send for them to his bed in turn, as it pleased him; the wives also, naturally.' He then related the tale of one of the daughters, a strong young woman who determined to have a lover of her own choice, 'and used to carry him in on her shoulders in the snow, so that there should be only one set of footprints inside the *Staket* instead of two, to deceive the giant emperor.' The *Fräulein* did not understand, as was proper, and stared at him with wide grey-green eyes. She was wearing gloves, and he assumed that she was the Ritter's daughter.

The history of the emperor and his female progeny heartened Gareth; the man who had been crowned Holy Roman Emperor had committed *incesta* like himself. That night he downed *schnapps* in the hotel bar and then went up and coupled with Sabrina enjoyably till morning. She kissed and hugged him, writhing suitably at the climaxes. Papa was getting good at it, almost as good as the young man with the zither.

Gareth finally slept against her, having decided that she should become his princess in an ivory tower, his own created *Staket*. To possess her frequently, incessantly, perhaps totally, must be made possible. He must confide in Pilar, who was trustworthy.

They set out at last for England, arriving back at Leys by spring.

\*     \*     \*

Sabrina was moderately pleased to be home, although it had been a variety to see all the places and people she had. She found Brian Laracor grown into a stranger, with stiff manners and a pink hunting-coat which he changed by lunch-time. He'd never liked her much, or she him. That time Pilar had caned her, and she'd had to stand for breakfast next day, he hadn't shown interest or sympathy, only looked down his nose.

By afternoon she had gone out to feed the waterfowl on the small lake with cake crumbs from tea; and stood there, watching the elegant swans and fussy moorhens and ducks, bustling and sending the surface in to sideways ripples the way they always had; and the aloof peacocks, trailing further off and taking nothing to do with anybody, not even their hen.

Beyond the peacocks, standing by himself, was Stevens. He was looking at her in a way that showed he remembered everything he'd done to her from a child. It was his fault she was like she was, having to be caned by Pilar. It would happen again if Pilar knew what was taking place with Papa. Pilar had been in love with Papa for years. Sabrina had noticed, but Papa didn't.

She pretended not to notice Stevens either, and instead turned and went in. It had begun to rain and she shed her wet clothes and shoes inside, leaving them in a heap for the servants. Then she changed into a shimmering grey gown Papa had bought for her in Zürich, and went down, her hair coiled becomingly high at the back of her neck. Once there, she found a piece of paper and wrote STEVENS on it, and handed it to Pilar. Pilar had horsewhipped Stevens once, while she herself had watched from the old coach where they'd been together. Watching had been entertaining. She didn't want Stevens again now she knew better. Pilar would see to it that he was sent away.

On seeing the note Pilar went to Brian Laracor, who did not seem perturbed. 'I got him work at the hunt kennels,' he said. 'He seems able enough.'

'Well, tell him not to show his face down here.' It was as much as she could do; after all Stevens couldn't be prevented from existing. Nevertheless the need to keep Sabrina out of his way, to make some arrangements that would take her well out of reach, was advisable, but the young squire wouldn't see it.

At dinner, Gareth admired the Zürich gown, and smiled across the table. To annoy Pilar—she was aware of her own power in such ways, and gloried in it—Sabrina rose and went to sit in Gareth's lap, giving him childlike butterfly kisses and running her fingers over his face to make him laugh. Pilar and Brian both looked sour. It wasn't the way to behave at table.

In fact they were both aware of the difference in Sabrina. She had left as a nymph, and now had returned as a goddess. She was the most beautiful creature they had ever seen, except for Stella; and Stella's blue-eyed, blue-gowned portrait hung where they could look at it as they dined. It was as though she was still among them.

The talk was desultory. What was there to say, apart from asking about the travels? Talk about travel by others comes to an end, and a silent Sabrina could contribute nothing unless visually. By half-past eight, Brian announced that he was going out to see that the grooms had remembered to put blankets on the horses lately out at grass; the rain had worsened. He departed, and soon Sabrina yawned and made towards bed. The rain began to hurl against the walls and windows; it would be pitting and peaking the surface of the lake, making little waves.

\*     \*     \*

During the night Pilar recalled that she might not have shut the drawing-room window; the carpet would be soaked. Gaining the passage, she saw a white-and-gold phantom; Sabrina, gliding out of Gareth's room back towards her own. Pilar clenched her fists and on shutting the window, went to her broom-cupboard and selected a short rod from the pickle-bucket. There were things she couldn't endure, and tomorrow, for his own sake, she would show Sir Gareth the sheriff's letter.

She climbed the stairs to Sabrina's room, and opened the door; the lamp was still lit. The young woman had taken off her bed-gown and was standing admiring her own naked body in front of the cheval-glass. Pilar, small but terrible as an army with banners, strode over and seized the shining hair, wound it round her left hand, then pulled the owner by it face down on her bed. Thereafter she whipped Sabrina soundly. Little bitch, little whore, enticing the man she thought was her father! What was more, she was pregnant; you could tell in the early stages, the nipples darkened. She probably didn't know yet herself.

The birch did its duty, with the rain still battering at the walls and drowning Sabrina's cries. The peach-smooth curves of her bottom, miraculously free of scars from Stella's childhood chastisements, began to rise in ugly weals. It was the third time Pilar's Spanish heritage had come out in uncontrollable and vicious strength. Yes, you can make yourself heard when you howl, young madam; lucky for you it isn't the cart's tail.

Leaving the sobbing and chastised goddess lying face down, Pilar locked the door behind her. That had been a good job of work and she didn't regret it. Tomorrow she'd tell Sir Gareth the truth. Miss Sabrina wasn't his daughter, and the choice thereafter was his.

* * *

She faced Gareth next day in his office, having asked for a private word. The sounds of the hunt had died away in the distance, and it was quiet. He looked up at her with the usual unseeing gaze. 'Where is Sabrina?' he asked. 'She did not come down to breakfast.'

'She did not come down because I've seen to it that she won't sit for a long time. There are things you should know, though I've tried to keep them from you.'

She left him with the letter, having already taken up a tray of coffee and rolls to a sullen Sabrina, still lying naked on her face. The weals on her bottom had turned scarlet and were beginning to subside. Neither of them had broken the silence, and Pilar had locked the door again. Young madam had her chamber-pot if she needed it. One day soon she'd start being sick into it, and wonder why.

Pilar waited while Gareth must have had time to read the contents of the envelope;

when she ventured into the study after that it was empty, and there was burning ash in the grate. Well, there it was; he knew. The next thing was, he'd try to do himself harm. She went to the gun-room. He was there, with a pistol balanced between his hands, a dazed expression on his face.

'Are you sure you've got the right gun?' Pilar asked him. 'Don't use any of 'em. Your life's of value to some, if not to yourself.'

His eyes gazed at her unseeingly. He never really had seen her. Tears had begun to dry on his cheeks, leaving furrows. He hadn't had much to laugh about since Stella died, she was thinking. Everyone needs laughter. She hadn't had much herself.

'Go to Raheere,' she told him. 'They need you there. Since old Dan died they're all at sixes and sevens; they kept sending word here while you were away. You can put 'em right, the way they used to be when you started up. Forget yourself and think of them.' She nearly said Stella would have wanted it, then didn't; Stella had only wanted what suited herself.

She went and took the gun gently from him. 'Come away from here,' she said. 'I'll see your things packed and a hot meal inside you before you go off. The rain's stopped.'

He turned, like a child, and obeyed her. He only said one thing; he didn't want to see Sabrina. That apart, she needn't worry about him. Once he was back at Raheere he would find enough to do. Keeping busy was the main thing. She went to clear the supper dishes from the table. He would no doubt stay at an inn on the way to the Welsh port.

She was in agony of mind for a long time about him; no word had come. However they would have heard by now if he hadn't got to Ireland. After some weeks a letter came, addressed to herself and unsigned.

*You did right to tell me. It is always best to know the truth. I leave everyone and everything in your charge at Leys.*

That meant he wouldn't be back. He ended by asking her to take down Stella's portrait and ship it across. He must want, once again, to look into the blue eyes.

Brian Laracor had had himself sketched in pastels in hunting gear, and Pilar hung that up in the missing place. The countenance of the long-dead Sir Eldred was still hung in the entrance hall, the first thing anyone saw.

She, Pilar, had done her duty. Now it only remained to finish what was left of her life. *Everyone and everything* had included Sabrina, but by then Pilar had known the latter must not continue at Leys. A life of her own was just possible if a certain plan came to fruition.

\*     \*     \*

She had taken a chastened Sabrina—the criss-cross marks still hadn't entirely faded—up to the correction-house in Leys carriage. Sabrina was looking as puritanical as possible in a lilac bonnet with strings tied under her chin, plain gown to match, and her hands encased in white gloves. Brian Laracor, by request, held the reins. Pilar had already explained part of the situation to him; he would never understand all of it, or want to.

'She is not your sister. You didn't have the same mother or the same father. Let that be enough, and don't ask questions.' He accepted, and supposed he had always done, the position Pilar occupied in the household, somewhat above that of a servant; what she said must, after all, be heeded. He had never had any affection for Sabrina; other fellows had sisters who could talk, not that what they had to say interested him. All he asked was to be allowed to live his life with the minimum of disturbance and oddity, and if Sabrina was about to be settled for life elsewhere it suited him perfectly well. Pilar knew what she was doing.

In fact Henry Yeoman himself came to take the horses' heads. Like most Australians, and the Golden Horde, he could do anything with a horse and most things with a woman. He resembled his uncle the late sheriff in all physical ways except that his eyes were red-brown, those of the long-vanished sea-captain.

His hair was a decent light brown, close-shaven.

He opened the carriage door as Pilar and Sabrina got out. He was already eyeing Sabrina as most men did, with a mixture of incredulity and lust. In her turn, she smiled at him divinely. Pilar had the feeling that everything was going to turn out as she had hoped.


## CHAPTER NINE

'I am prepared to pay your fare back to Australia, Mr Yeoman, and that of Sabrina here, and to make a small settlement on you both, provided you agree to marry her. You must understand that she is deaf and dumb and that she may be in trouble, having been unable to protect herself.'

That was the way she'd rehearsed it; it gave Sabrina a chance to make a fresh start, as they called it. She herself could afford the money out of what Sir Gareth had paid her at the time of Brian's birth. She hadn't really done anything with it. However Henry spoke up and said he didn't need the money, he could support a wife, and blokes within forty miles of Parramatta would give their ears for one who couldn't answer back. 'If she gives trouble I'll wallop her,' he said absently. He had scarcely taken his eyes off Sabrina, who was still smiling.

All that was needed in the sectarian ceremony were two witnesses. When a ring was required Pilar produced the one she'd made Sabrina take off her finger at the beginning; it hadn't been strictly needed until now.

After the vows had been exchanged, with the bride nodding instead of speaking, Sabrina leaned over of her own accord and kissed Henry Yeoman full on the mouth. His homely face was transmogrified, flesh calling to flesh. They could hardly wait to get into bed. The carriage was returned containing only Pilar, with her son at the reins, to Leys House.

Sabrina's subsequent history drifted back home now and again. On the voyage it was noted that she was pregnant, and almost at once on arrival at Parramatta she gave birth to a black-haired son. As soon as she was fit Yeoman walloped her, saying with truth it wasn't his and she had better learn. In both assumptions he was correct; the sire was the briefly encountered zither player behind the dais at the Swiss chalet. This boy grew up with a remarkable baritone voice, was spotted early by a talent-manager, and toured the world singing, sending home money to his beautiful speechless mother and brothers and, by then, half-brothers. Yeoman had given Sabrina a child a year till he died when a horse pecked at the gallop, throwing him: in the manner of his death, if no more, he resembled Sabrina's half-brother. Sabrina married again and again, and yet again. Her fourth husband, a chemist of Dutch extraction, was the only one not to give her children, understandably as both partners were by then in their sixties. Sabrina lived to a ripe old age and when she died, was given a cheerful funeral attended by Highland pipers, as is the Australian custom. Her tombstone was of grey granite and bore the inscription IN LOVING MEMORY OF OUR DEAREST MOTHER SABRINA VANDERHUIS, DIED AT A RIPE AGE, SADLY MISSED. No dates were put on as nobody was entirely certain when and where the old lady had first seen the light, and there was no one left alive to explain. It was known that most of the sons had had voracious testicles and had multiplied exceedingly, as had the daughters. None of them were deaf.

## CHAPTER TEN

Pilar's life had continued less eventfully. Day followed day, in the way it had for many years now, going the rounds of the house, seeing that everything was kept clean, fresh and polished, the silver shining, the crystal gleaming, all Miss Stella's cherished things in their place, Sir Eldred's portrait dusted where it hung in the hall. She prayed constantly for Gareth, and it was as though her prayers reached out and brought him aid; the Laracor products were beginning to recover their former reputation for quality and long wear, and were in demand through the civilised world. The *Tribune* flourished although she herself seldom read it; she wasn't a reader, she preferred to listen to others' talk and keep things in her head, or else knit when everything else was done for the day.

The news about Laracor she had from Brian her son of the name, idly as though it didn't concern him; trade was trade. He was slightly ashamed of his father, who mixed with the wrong people. As for Pilar, she continued to be treated by him with deference for a reason he still didn't fully grasp; it must be her long connection with the house. She was ironically aware of this situation, and had she had more in common with the withdrawn young man might have been troubled. As it was, she led her own life in her own way and left Brian Laracor to do likewise.

One day she saw him ride off as usual to the hunt. It was a winter's morning and the pond was thin with ice. Brian Laracor's pink coat showed up well against the bare dark skeletons of the trees. With any other son she would have called out to him to be careful how he went; the ground was slippery with frost and he was riding a new hunter. However it was useless to tell Brian Laracor anything; he knew it already.

She watched him ride into the distance, faintly dulled with the fog that can later mean snow; and for a time looked out for the streak of doomed flame, the fox, but they'd gone another way. Pilar returned to her usual tasks, finally going upstairs to polish a looking-glass that had often reflected Stella's lovely face. By contrast her own was as unremarkable as ever; one benefit of that was that it had changed very little from what it had ever been, except that her black hair had turned grey as iron. She hardly ever troubled to look at herself; it wasn't worth the elaborate frame to do so.

Descending again, she could hear the sounds of arrival outside. There were seldom visitors except for the hunting fraternity, at present out and away in the nature of things. Perhaps it was old Abigail Comstock, who came down now and again to unburden herself of overloaded secrets. She knew they didn't go any further.

It wasn't Abigail. It was an ashen-faced young man who had ridden out with the pack that morning. He was the second son of the dedicated huntswoman who had irritated Stella long ago. He stammered out that it was bad news. Pilar knew at once that her son was dead. If he had only been hurt, they would have brought him home.

'What happened?' she heard herself asking. She still felt nothing, not even when she heard that the new hunter had failed at a jump, had slipped on ice, and had fallen, breaking its leg and its rider's neck. They would bring him home later, the boy said. The hunter had been shot. The leg wouldn't have mended.

She heard herself say, 'A telegram must be sent to his father.'

When they brought the body home, covered in a sheet, she peeled it away and looked down on her son's dead face. This should have been a moment of great anguish, but she still felt nothing. The face was Gareth's, dead. The neck was awry and she was reminded of the little dog Talley whose spine had been broken in Dublin long ago, and whose head had lolled against her. Why think of that now? She had loved the dog, but she hadn't been allowed to love her son. Now it was too late. He had been taken away from her, had never belonged to her. More than his birth she remembered his conception; and that memory comforted her. That was hers for always.

She covered up the dead face, and waited for the coffin, the mourners, the condolences, the funeral. It was the funeral of the last squire of Leys. On the day of the burial, the passing-bell tolled once each minute for the hours between seven and noon. It had always been the custom. Gareth still hadn't arrived.

He hadn't sent word. He must be

somewhere else. She knew that her heart would tell her if there had been harm, death, or accident to him. He must be somewhere else; and he hadn't, after all, greatly loved Brian Laracor; nobody had but Brian himself. Perhaps that was what had made the young man self-centred, having of necessity to love himself, lacking other love or the ability to gain it.

It was too late. Everything was too late. The procession started, and wound off without her.

They interred the last squire of Leys in the ugly vault beside Sir Eldred and his estranged widow. There was no more room, as if it had been foreseen that the line of old Sir Posthumus Seaborne would not endure longer than two centuries. Perhaps it was Old Noll's revenge, at last, for the well-aimed brick. At first the townsfolk were out in their blacks, but secretly glad; with the passing of the last squire, the inheritance would be theirs. Nevertheless the death-bell tolled.

\* \* \*

Two days later, a delegation came from the town council. They asked Pilar formally if she would continue to keep the great house as a museum on behalf of the people of Leys. There had been a meeting at which it had been decided that the antique coach in which the late Sir Eldred had been driven about his avocations, to the sound of beaten ploughshares and braying trumpets, should be placed in a glass container in the entrance hall, along with such evidence of the ancient practice as remained. 'You have kept the house remarkably well,' the new high sheriff told Pilar. 'We could find nobody more suitable, if you will agree to the salary.'

He named it. Everything had been decided already. They didn't let the grass grow under their feet.

## CHAPTER ELEVEN

She began to take up her new life as a salaried servant of the town council. In most ways it was the same; they didn't disturb her except for the occasional need for modifying of a private house into a museum. It had been decided that the statue of Sir Eldred, which was a condition of the legacy, should stand not in the market square, its site already occupied by the late sheriff's Ionian marble phallus, but beyond the pond in Leys garden itself. A sculptor was employed and there was much coming and going, the waterfowl were disturbed and to Pilar's anger, somebody stole two swans to roast for Christmas. The ducks began to go as well. She couldn't keep an eye everywhere, and the council said they'd appoint a man to guard the premises, inside and out.

The man they selected was Stevens.

She supposed they had their reasons; he'd been employed about the place for many years, the MFH himself had given him a reference as having been reliable up at the kennels, and he was getting older now and couldn't walk the hounds the way he was used to doing. It had been odd to see him among the hunt mourners assembling for Brian Laracor's funeral, and proved how little she'd had to do with her own son that Sabrina's childhood seducer should follow his coffin as a close acquaintance.

Still, it was a different matter to think of him leering at the coach in its glass case, remembering what had happened in it. She sent in her resignation, not making it clear why. She had enough money of her own to take a little house in town, and leave Leys and its memories before they were further spoilt. The council expressed its regret, and appointed Abigail. They could, again, have done worse.

'You're welcome down here any time,' said Abigail graciously, bridling at her new importance. However Pilar knew she would never go back. She had her few things moved up to town, took to shopping every day, gazing in the windows, walking past, sometimes seeing her own reflection beyond the stacked displayed wares of bakers, confectioners, sellers of everyday china, ironmongers. It passed the time. Otherwise she would see to her small house, and knit. She didn't keep a servant, although she could have afforded one. Servants chattered. Pilar liked silence about her affairs, such as they were.

However one day a white-haired man got out of a carriage in the street below. Her heart leaped. She hadn't supposed she would ever see Sir Gareth again.

\*       \*       \*

'Have you dined?' was all she could find to say. He gestured it aside, laying his tall hat on the table. She could see that the white hair was still thick. He'd changed very little, really, from last time. He turned to her and looked at her steadily, then sat down.

'I have looked at a portrait for many years,' he said. 'A portrait can bring comfort, but not love. I am a lonely man. I read a great deal.'

'What do you read, besides the paper?' she enquired politely. She didn't really mind what he read. It was like a visitation from an angel to have him sitting there, talking to her at last as if she was a person, someone he noticed. She had seated herself in the chair opposite, her hands folded in her lap. This would be an hour to cherish. She supposed he'd been passing, for some reason, and had called in for old times' sake. Old times. Their son had been buried five years, and he'd never written.

He had answered her meantime. 'I read poetry,' he said. 'I used to try to write it when I was young. I was a young man full of ideals, and some have become reality, though not all. I can remember one line of poetry, not mine, as I sit here; *one far fierce hour and sweet.* You can recall it. I did not permit myself to do so for many years, first because of Stella, then because at her death you thrust a golden-haired child into my arms. If you had not done so, I might have fallen into yours.'

She was silent. He had never spoken like this before. *One far fierce hour.* She knew the fire still burned in her. It hadn't ever gone out. What he said next almost made her head spin. It was sudden, after so many years; it must have lain about somewhere in the back of his own mind, but he hadn't said anything.

'Pilar, will you marry me and come back to Ireland? I sit by my fireside night after night, with nothing but the portrait on the wall. I need your love,' he said. 'We could play chess.' He smiled reminiscently, then grew grave again. 'I think you have always felt it. Had you not done so you would have left, married, not stayed through everything to remain a prop and stay. I didn't come to Brian Laracor's funeral; I was too greatly ashamed. I had never been a father to him.'

'I was never allowed to become a mother to

him. That was what was wrong with him. Oh, I dare say he might have married somebody in the end, for the sake of the inheritance, but as it was he didn't seem to fancy anybody.' She was looking down at her fingers, worn as they were with work. 'Why don't you marry Mrs Duveen?' she asked; she had always, now the cards were on the table, been jealous of that lady, who'd been able to feed and look after him for years. At least she'd taught Sabrina to cook and make herself useful; Henry Yeoman would feel the benefit.

'I should think I'd get in her way,' Gareth smiled. 'You have not answered my proposal, and I will make it a second time. Will you become my wife, Pilar?' He was looking at her now with great intentness. She still temporised, and didn't know why; it was still sudden; when had he decided to arrive today'?

'I don't know that I could live up to it,' she said. 'I'm not a lady. My mother ran off with somebody else and my father put me into the orphanage when he was dying. After that there wasn't much finery, till I came to Leys.' She remembered Mr Greenbody, and his upholstered wife in her drawing-room, and the hay cart, and lying all night in the Dublin office doorway. It had all led to a great many things. It had all led to this; this, at last, and from the beginning she'd loved him.

'You have the gift of silence,' he said. 'I think I have always loved you in my heart, without daring to admit it to my mind. If you will not marry me, and come and look after me, I shall be desolate. I shall soon die, because there is nothing left for which to live: there's an editor for the paper, a manager for the shop. I need you. I have known it now for years. Is it because of Sabrina that you are unwilling? She's happy. You say I did not commit incest. Nevertheless I thought I was doing so, and they say the thought is what counts. If she hadn't looked like Stella, it would never have happened.'

'I know you loved Stella, and she loved you. If you'd continued to be a husband to her, other things wouldn't have happened either, or not after the first. You know all that.'

'I know all that. When you told me Sabrina was not my daughter, not my flesh and Stella's, but that and that other's, I didn't want to see Sabrina again.'

'I don't think you ever loved Sabrina,' she said slowly. 'It was like that doll you once bought her. It was the same to look at, but not the same inside.'

'So, I have to propose to you three times?' he said. 'Lacking you, as I say, there is nothing left.' He was beginning to look perturbed, as though something had gone badly wrong.

'You old fool, why have you taken all these years to say so?' she replied, and went over and took both his hands. She wouldn't mind Stella's portrait, left on the wall.

We hope you have enjoyed this Large Print book. Other Chivers Press or Thorndike Press Large Print books are available at your library or directly from the publishers.

For more information about current and forthcoming titles, please call or write, without obligation, to:

Chivers Large Print
published by BBC Audiobooks Ltd
St James House, The Square
Lower Bristol Road
Bath  BA2 3BH
UK
email: bbcaudiobooks@bbc.co.uk
www.bbcaudiobooks.co.uk

OR

Thorndike Press
295 Kennedy Memorial Drive
Waterville
Maine 04901
USA
www.gale.com/thorndike
www.gale.com/wheeler

All our Large Print titles are designed for easy reading, and all our books are made to last.